WHEN YOU'RE GONE

AMIT SHARMA

Invincible Publishers

First published in India in 2018

ISBN: 978-93-88333-09-2

Invincible Publishers

G-120, Sushant Lok III, Sector 57, Gurgaon-122002

Registered Address: Opposite Kasturba Ashram, Radaur, Haryana–135133

Printed at Thomson Press (India) LTD

For you, a thousand times over.

-Khaled Hosseini

Acknowledgement

A few clarifications before I give thanks. This is not my story in any way, as people always inquire every time I write a story, especially a love story, and it is purely a work of fiction. Though, those who are familiar with my life will notice that I have always taken minor liberties to take instances from my own life to sketch out the central character or the people I come across and draw inspiration from them. Also, to give the story authenticity, I have used names of real places as they always aid in storytelling. The essence always stays in telling the truth and beauty of these places and people living there.

This book actually began as a big, messy thing three years ago and required more than just patience and sleepless nights to chisel something comprehensible out of this story.

With this, I would like to thank my managing editor, Ajay Setia, who guided me right from the editing process till the publication of this book. His guidance was indispensable. My publication manager, Anjali Arya, for her patience and support; my editors, Aditi Saxena and Dhwani Swadia for editing the story as much as it was required; my designer, Ashish Samant, for his understanding and designing the cover the way I wished, along with the marketing head, Ruhani Alwadhi who's contribution is just as crucial as writing and editing the book.

Over the years, my friends mocked me for using vocabulary which at times was not easy to comprehend, as in the previous works of mine. And therefore, I would like to extend my thanks to my friend, Nidhi Vashisht, who was forthright and sincere to let me know that the book needed some relevant changes in the beginning of the story itself. I thank her for being up-front in telling me that. For this book, I've taken every possible feedback from my friends–Kanika Gera, Suman Saini, Avni Seth, Neha Sharma and Syed Misbah, and I thank all of them for letting me know even the most minuscule of grammatical and narrative errors. I further extend my thanks to Komal Narang for helping me out in suggesting a suitable title for this book. It was the toughest part for me, you'd agree to.

A very special gratitude goes out to my brother, Anand Sharma, for being a silent enthusiast always for my books, and my friends, Bharat Malik and Rachna Chhillar, for their appreciation for my work has been unspoken over the years. I am also grateful to my friends–Amit Chamoli, Neeraj Joshi, Suraj Upadhyay, Sandeep Vashisht and Navneet Pandey for their constant buttress throughout my writing journey. You guys have been rock solid and gladly, nothing has ever changed between us. Also, I never doubt the existence of mutual love and respect between us.

To Rohan Singhal, for being a friend who has given me the access to his small library and never saying no whenever I needed a book for a research; Gaurav Kumar, for being a friend who was always supportive towards my work and doing the amazing work as a designer. You've been a great help in last three years. In addition to my long list of thanksgiving, I would also like to thank Lionel Richie and Akshay Chopra, without whom this book would have been completed a little earlier. But jokes apart, you two have been with me through thick and thin in the last two years, and I thank you both for being a friend whenever I needed one the most.

Lastly, my sincerest gratitude to my father, Ashok Sharma, from whom I inherited being honest in my life in whatever I chose to do, and my mother, Meena Sharma, for her love, trust and unwavering faith in me. I remain indebted and grateful to both of you. You made this possible.

Prologue

Amman is on the brink of change. He says he's done with the romantic genre. So, what will happen next? He cannot say, but he believes something new will happen.

"I know this reinvention phase will take time, but I will take a break for now."

I ask him why he's trying to change the genre he has found success in, to which he says, "I have so many stories to tell and I have all these ideas, but I had no idea what to do with them some days ago. I've written everything I wanted to through my trilogy, especially about love."

The book…I look at it lying on the table. Amman hands it to me. I glance at the dedication page.

To the two angels of my life: My mother, Zarina, and the love of my life, Noor. I owe you both everything.

"Have you read the previous ones?" Amman asks.

"No."

"Ah."

"I'm going to read them now, although I'm not a voracious reader. I guess it's my turn to pick one."

Amman smiles. I ask him if he ever reads his own work after it gets published. He refuses. It's true. He has not read his own work and doubts if he ever will. He does not think he has the stomach to revisit himself on its pages, but others will. I ask him why he does not do interviews, he tells me, "People will know everything about me, I find that boring."

I open the book again. Just then, his phone beeps, probably for the twentieth time since I entered his hotel room.

"Congratulatory messages!" Amman says. "I'll keep it on silent mode for now."

I suppose he should be relieved, but a part of him wishes for something else.

"I hope everything's okay."

"Yes, of course."

I nod nonchalantly.

"You understand why we are here, Amman?"

"Yes, I understand."

He gets up and closes the door that I had left open. He comes back and sits again. We begin.

*****

Excerpt From an Interview

With Amman by Jennifer Kohl,

(Magneto), P.25

JK: So, I understand you were not always living in London?

A: I grew up here, in India. My mother raised me singlehandedly. I went to London only five years ago.

JK: So, you started your writing journey in London, not in India?

A: Yes.

JK: And I've heard that you were a travel writer before this. Why this change of profession?

We are sitting in Amman's room on the fourth floor at a hotel in New Delhi. The room is not very big, but is well-lit and sparsely decorated: a green-upholstered couch, a coffee table and us. Amman sits with his back to the window, which is closed and well-covered with elegant curtains.

Amman states that his age is thirty-two. He comes across as a handsome guy, but if you mention this to him, he objects saying he has never been told so before by anyone. I tell him that he's still young and quite successful at this age. He has this charming smile on his face and is wearing a beige colored blazer with torn blue jeans and off-white sneakers. It was only ten thirty in the morning when I arrived at his room, and to his kind nature, he poured me a hot cup of tea. The taste of the tea brought me back to my childhood when I was around nine.

A: I know. Earlier, I was writing accounts of my real-life experiences while traveling all around India, and now I write everything fictional. But I'm still writing.

JK: Are you writing something from your own life?

A: Ah…not exactly.

JK: I'm curious as to what this *not exactly* means!

A: I think it's obvious. Since you must have interviewed many people in your life, mostly artists, you'd know that it's impossible to figure out their true being. You'll always find their story reflected in their work.

JK: What about you?

A: The answer is as vexing as it is predictable, but this is only applicable to a very small part of my life.

JK: So, it's true! Love touched *your* heart as well.

A: I think it comes to everybody's life.

JK: I think the reverse is equally true.

A: I wouldn't agree to that. I believe it's about accepting the love that comes your way, irrespective of whether you're ready for it or not.

JK: And how did your shift to London happen?

A: It happened sometime after my mother died. I had no one to fall back on…no close relatives.

JK: But you *did* visit Paris once, right before you went to London…did you go there to see someone?

He smiles and shrugs. *Yes.* He answers.

JK: And you met that person there?

He nods.

JK: And how did all this happen? First India, then Paris, and then London…and now we're sitting here for the interview.

A: My journey took me to all these places.

I ask him to elaborate.

CHAPTER 1

Two weeks ago

London

"Jenny, Pete's calling you inside. Now!" A woman carrying some papers came and said stiffly, "I think he wants an update about the story he's asked you to work on."

"What, now?"

"You'll find out only when you go," she said and walked off to her cubicle.

It was eleven thirty and Jennifer was sitting in her cubicle, looking at her laptop screen. She was going through an interview she had done with a rock band a month ago. Her phone beeped just then. She read the message, '*Come now, if convenient.*' The message was from Peter, the editor-in-chief, but she ignored it and went back to the interview video again. A coffee mug on her table had been going cold for the last thirty minutes, but she didn't have the time to take even a sip. She laughed at herself and wondered how dull her life had become. When she counted all the distress she had taken for this job, she realized she had not had even a pinch of happiness in her world. She placed her laptop furiously on the table and shrugged. It seemed like it had been ages since she smiled at something beautiful or laughed at something natural. She had not taken a vacation for nearly three years and thought what a bore her life had become. This was not how it was supposed to be.

Her phone beeped again. '*Now!*'

She closed her eyes for a moment and took a deep breath. It was obvious now why she was being called. She grabbed her cell-phone and left her cubicle to walk into Peter's cabin. The clamor at the back office was enough to put her into a state of sullenness.

"*What is so annoying today?*" she thought. What was it that had left such a void in her life?

"For how long did you plan to keep ignoring my messages?" Peter asked as she entered his cabin.

She stood there lamely, her hair left loose over her shoulders and her fragile looking slender figure unassuming of the cunning eyes that stared at Peter.

"What is it now? Why does it take one person and two texts for you to come to my cabin?"

"Bored!" she said.

"Just?"

"Is this what you really wanted to say now, Peter?" she retorted.

"Come. Sit here," Peter motioned towards a chair with his hand and grabbed another one for himself. "Come on, Jenny. Sit."

She walked stubbornly and sat opposite his editorial desk.

"I don't understand your obstinacy. You don't look the same as yesterday. These are really not your colors. Is everything…"

"Everything's absolutely fine," she interrupted. "I'm sure I'm here for a reason."

"Well, I'm sending you somewhere to cover a story."

"Where?" She looked at him coolly.

"I need you to interview someone. Someone on whom we're doing a story for this month's edition of *Magneto*. I know you're best suited for this job as you know what I want out of it." Peter scratched his forehead and smiled gravely. He looked at his laptop and began typing, brows furrowed as if the work he was doing was of utmost importance. Jennifer sat motionless, as if this interview was the last thing in the world she would do. She felt like she was sitting in a closed chamber, with the ambiance of the office strangulating her. The news didn't give her the joy of visiting a new place, meeting someone new and doing what she was best at. She felt tired of this mundane life.

"And what do you want out of it?" she asked in a manner and tone that sounded interrogative and unpleasant. "Where am I going? And who am I to interview?"

"Amman, the writer. We're carrying a story on him for this month's issue. So, I'm sending you to India."

"India?" Jennifer casted a skeptical glance at him.

"Yeah, what's wrong? That's what your job is, no?" Peter looked at her obliquely.

"It is."

"Why do you look so stressed? What's wrong, Jenny?" Peter glanced at her, worried that this tease, albeit a little reckless and unnecessary, might have offended her. "I don't see you all that lively today, what is on your mind?" He asked eventually, keeping his laptop aside.

"You're sending me all the way to India just to interview some writer?" Jennifer said sharply.

"If you've something better planned, let me know." Peter looked at her gravely.

"Can't we do this interview over the phone, Peter? Why is it so necessary for me to fly all the way to India and get some god-damn story of a writer?"

"I'm not asking you to ask him a few questions regarding his well-being or how it is to write. We're carrying a story on him–a full-fledged cover story for our month's edition. That's what our job is. Suppress this ego of yours and start digging," he said in a commanding voice. But to Jennifer, the reason was still very vague. She tried to comprehend this order, but it was in vain. The story didn't seem all that worthy to her.

"You know, you're trying too hard, Jenny. Just keep calm, it's only an interview. You'll only be doing your job and you'll get paid for it. So, let's drop this act and get to work."

Her mouth had gone dry. "I'm trying to," she said.

Peter stared at her for a moment, then spoke mildly, "Take a break after this. You need it. Go somewhere and spend a week or so with your family… and please, stop being so puerile."

She sighed at last. "When do I leave? And how am I supposed to meet him?"

"He will be in New Delhi after a couple of days. When you reach India, you'll meet a man named Zafar Ali. He'll be your lead and let you know the easiest way to get to Amman. I'll give you all the details by this evening," he said and paused for a while. "Jenny, what happened to you?" Peter asked, his voice finally betraying the concern he felt.

She looked at him with full composure and said, "Nothing happened to me." She then got up and left his office.

She had been working for Magneto for three years. It was a magazine firm based in London. In the time that she worked here, she had interviewed various artists from all walks of life, be it painters, movie stars, rock stars, or architects; almost everyone who was well known in his/her field. She had earned a place for herself as a tireless hard worker of the firm. She really enjoyed her job and counted on the support of her widowed mother. She loved to travel to different places, meet people and know the stories behind their work, and the madness and thrill that came with it. It was the joy she felt that motivated her, which had begun to die in her of late. She had been trying to get back to her usual self for the last few weeks, rather a month, but had failed. Her colleagues often asked her about her sudden change in conduct, but she kept quiet, or changed the subject, or sometimes even walked away. She didn't know what to do and just wanted to escape the monotony that had recently set in her life.

As promised, the details of the interview lay on her desk that evening. She had to leave for India in two days. Her heart began to palpitate. Perhaps, it was a presentiment of something bad. She raced back home, had her dinner, watched television, and ate popcorn to kill the dullness. That night, she slept for nearly twelve hours and when she woke up, she didn't feel like getting up from the bed or going to work. So, she didn't. She informed Peter that she wanted a day off from work before leaving for India.

She persuaded herself that she would start her journey on a cheerful note, just as she used to before, but the sadness would not go away. The work she loved doing the most had somehow lost its charm. She knew she needed a reason, a purpose, to continue her job and her life as an interviewer. She missed something, but without pondering over it for too long, she packed her bag and left for India. She had made it quite clear to Peter that she needed no one to accompany her and wanted to be left alone so she could appreciate and take delight in what she was good at. She had spent enough time thinking about herself. She needn't go beyond the fact that she was lonely and hollow. There was a sense of derangement in how she felt about herself. She laughed and nudged all those thoughts away, carrying on the mission entrusted unto her.

When her flight landed at IGI airport, New Delhi, she felt ecstatic. The fresh morning breeze seemed delightful, and the shimmering sunlight mixed with the cool weather embosomed her. She was overjoyed and uttered, "Good riddance," to London's boring weather.

It was Jennifer's first official visit to India and she knew how difficult it was going to be for her here, since she was all alone too. She cherished the memory of visiting her maternal grandfather in New Delhi as a kid. Her mother originally belonged to this place, while her father was from London. She had come back after twelve long years on an assignment that she had reluctantly taken. Earlier, it seemed like a pitfall which she had no interest in jumping into, but now she felt placid just to be on Indian soil again. A thousand memories from the past resurfaced and brought a jovial smile to her face. It was pacifying to finally be here, and she decided to stay on for a few days after her work. She had no idea how long it was going to take to meet Amman for the cover story, for one interview. She was jaded by the entire thing by now. She walked out of the airport to find a hotel, for her next step was to find Zafar–the man she had to meet first to dig deeper into Amman's story. The journey had begun.

She found a hotel for herself, but she had nobody with whom she could talk. In a nice cozy hotel room, she found herself doing nothing. She felt relaxed from the boring routine of her life. There were no phone calls, no orders, or deadlines. Nothing. She had one simple job to complete and she could explore as much as she wanted to after that. She found solace in a strange way in that snug hotel room and finally felt peace.

CHAPTER 2

Jennifer finally did meet Zafar. She had arrived alone, but had a lot of questions. She told him the purpose of their meeting and what she wanted to know. Zafar understood that he had been roped into this due to his friendship with Amman. The discomfort that usually overtook Jennifer in a situation like this was mitigated by Zafar's considerable ease. Jennifer found it amusing, even endearing, the way he openly talked about a lot of things with no embarrassment.

"So, you were with him in those days?" Jenny asked placidly.

"No, not at all," Zafar replied. "But I know a few things about him which might interest you."

Jennifer, dressed in her casuals and carrying a satchel over her shoulder, had come to meet Zafar at his restaurant. It was a cold winter morning and sitting in the nice and pleasant ambiance of the restaurant, she felt thoroughly relaxed. She had been to places all over the world, but she had never felt this relaxed before. She was at ease, and now her reliance was in the fact that she expected to amass as much information as possible about Amman from Zafar.

"What was he like…I mean…towards life or people?" Jennifer began with her customary question. Zafar had chosen to have them seated in a quiet corner where he could be more open and forthright to her queries. "My editor feels this is the most opportune time to bring out a story on him. His book is getting launched worldwide from London in a few days. And…"

"Well, you could've met him there itself," interrupted Zafar. "Why would someone come thousand miles away to cover a story on him?"

"Peter feels we must go back to his roots if we're bringing out a story on him in our next edition. He's someone who always wishes to bring out the soul in a story. What better way is there to know someone closely when you're writing a story and get to know everything about him from the beginning? His roots are here…in this place. It doesn't matter if he goes to London or New York, his soul is always going to be where his heart lies," Jennifer retorted.

"You speak fast…"

"Part of my job. Sometimes, I have to be spontaneous as well."

"I am afraid there's no special story around him. It's like any other story that one would come across. Time plays an imperative role in his story. Besides, I'm not sure how many people there are out there who'd be interested to know his story. He's not a celebrity and definitely not someone who remains in the public eye," Zafar said. Jennifer stayed silent for a moment, wondering where the conversation was heading. "But since you're here, miles away from home, it has to mean something and anything I say about him will be honest, real and true to his life, I assure you. I'll tell you every bit about him that I know."

"I expect exactly that from you," Jennifer said in a manner that was swayed by a sentiment she herself didn't understand fully.

"He was a wanderer. I had not expected to meet such a guy in my life. It was a chance meeting with him, else, how often do you meet people accidentally who leave an everlasting impression on you? But I also believe in the fact that it was on my insistence that a chance meeting with him converted into a long term friendship. About six or seven years ago, I met him in Darjeeling…" began Zafar. Jennifer brought out a diary from her satchel and began writing the account of Amman's life through the eyes of Zafar. She was curious now to know the tale narrated by Zafar. Somehow it felt strange, but that was perfectly okay with her. She had felt a similar way before interacting with artists from all over the world. Though it was nothing new to her, there was an amusing vivacity in her even after all these years.

"I was there on a vacation with my wife and kids sometime around July in monsoon. My wife and kids had persuaded me to visit Darjeeling and we had a great time, I must say. But I almost lost my little one there, you know. We were at Darjeeling's most auspicious Hindu temple, and we lost sight of him in the crowd there. We panicked; my wife, my elder son and I started running all over and amidst all this perplexity, I saw my son sitting with a stranger on the temple's stairs. He was sobbing, but this man had his arms around my son, trying to stop him from snivelling. That stranger was him. That's where I first met him by accident. We thanked him for being protective towards our son and went on. At first, he seemed like any other tourist there, but after two days, I saw him again," Zafar continued. "One day, while loitering in one of the tea estates, I found him with an employee of the tea estate."

"Did he see you?" Jennifer interrupted. Meanwhile, they were served tea and an assortment of sandwiches on the table.

"I waved to him the moment our eyes caught each other's gaze, but he turned away and continued talking to the guy. I didn't barge in. I kept strolling there for some time. I was alone that day. Then as of from nowhere, I got a pat on my back. I was amused to find him, for I thought he hadn't recognized me."

"But he did, right?"

"No. He didn't."

They both laughed at this. Jennifer was completely at ease now. Zafar poured tea for her while she gazed out of the window to view the panorama. It was nothing less than the bustling city of London. She kept staring outside and shrugged, disappointed. She could not bring herself to appreciate the mundane things outside, and shifted her gaze back in to look at the porcelain cup and saucer, and the lightings, trying to absorb herself back into the ambiance of the restaurant.

"Lost somewhere?" queried Zafar.

"Quite," she said as she glanced outside heedlessly again. "Nothing considerable though."

"Sure?"

"Pretty much." She paused and began, "So, what did he say when he came to you?"

"It was only a matter of a minute and we caught on. It was then that I learned he was a travel writer who stayed at various places for months to write about it, before going to another place. He was in Darjeeling for the same reason. His vivacity was infectious to me. And yes, to an extent I was mesmerized by his persona too. He had a tinge of a hypnotic personality. His energy was spot on. Frankly speaking, I liked the guy," Zafar said. "You know, he stood before me, carrying a backpack over his shoulder as if he was ready to leave for some new place. I have a very fond memory of that meeting." They talked as they ate.

Jennifer was inwardly flattered that Zafar recalled so much from the meeting that happened so many years before.

"I'm sorry I didn't recognize you!"

"Oh, but I haven't forget you. We met two days ago in that..."

"Temple, right? Now I absolutely remember you, sir. Nothing like meeting a stranger-cum-friend in an unknown place." They shared a laugh.

"I waved the moment I saw you, but I guess you didn't realize it, so I continued on my own way."

"Well, the tea estate guy was guiding me through this aromatic factory, talking about the process of withering, rolling, fermenting, and drying. He was explaining how green, black, and white teas come from the same leaf," Amman said.

"You seem to take special interest in tea!"

"Oh, not really! That's just part of my job."

I narrowed my eyes.

"I'm a travel writer. I travel, visit all sorts of places, gather information, and write about them."

"Sounds interesting!"

Amman smiled.

"No, really. You have an interesting job," I emphasized.

"Literally, I do. I enjoy every bit of my traveling. There's a bit of a nomad in me and I've chosen this nomadic life. What better way to enjoy life than traveling to places all over the world."

"And what great way to make new friends along the journey..." I said and shook hands with Amman. We shared a good camaraderie in that meeting. I felt Amman enjoyed meeting me, but he may have met many Zafars in his life. It didn't really matter for once when they met, for it was all momentary.

"And that's it?" Jennifer asked.

"That's it," Zafar said smiling.

"So how did you guys meet the next time? What brought you two together again?" Jennifer was not entirely pleased with the brief account that Zafar had put before her. It was nothing but paltry.

"So, by this time, I knew enough about him, where he was staying and where he was going next. I had this much information and we were strangers no more. He had told me then and there that his next destination was going to be my hometown, Shimla."

Jennifer kept writing everything she found imperative for the story in her diary.

"And he met you in Shimla again?"

"Soon! It took him a few months to visit the place, but in Darjeeling, I didn't see him again. I asked him to meet me in Shimla whenever his schedule allowed him to."

"It wasn't a very memorable meeting then, I suppose," Jennifer took a jibe.

"What else can one expect in the first meeting, that too from a stranger?"

"Indeed," Jennifer smiled and sipped her tea quietly with no further questions for few minutes. Though, she talked a bit about how the city had grown by leaps and bounds since her last visit, which was more than twelve years ago. Zafar spoke with no inhibitions and shared his own experiences in the city. The rendezvous kept going at a pleasant pace and Jennifer went back to the topic at hand.

"So, how did your second meeting happen with him?"

"In Shimla itself, and it went fine, but fate had brought him there for a different purpose this time. It changed everything for him forever." Zafar was suddenly solemn.

"In what way?" Jennifer asked, looking at him curiously. Zafar didn't speak for a moment. He had a vague look in his eyes, as if reminiscing the past, then he uttered, "He met Ayesha there–the girl he loved."

Jennifer shrugged at the mention of the word *love,* Zafar noticed this.

"What? What happened?" he asked, as he knitted his brows.

"Nothing!"

"No really, what happened?" he asked again.

"It's just love all the time, isn't it? All hearts are broken at the end…" A pained look flashed across her face.

Zafar nodded and asked, "Have you ever been in love?"

"How does that matter?" she responded annoyingly. Zafar could see the change in her conduct suddenly, but he didn't probe further.

"I didn't mean to pry."

"Of course, you didn't. It's just one of those things that keep coming back to me. She held her head in her hands, as if something was bothering her.

"Are you okay?" asked Zafar, wishing he'd talked of something else.

"I am. I am."

"You don't seem to be though. Tell me, how long are you going to be here?" He tried to change the course of their discussion.

"No really, I'm fine. It happens sometimes…"

"I insist that you stay here for a while," he interrupted. "We could have this discussion later. I'll tell you the remaining story then," he said calmly and added further, "and I promise to keep it light."

Jennifer looked at him obliquely and smiled. She wondered what had made her so vulnerable that she could not take the conversation ahead. She didn't speak about it further and left immediately.

She wondered why she had reacted so visibly. Back in her hotel room, she kept wondering about the perpetual change in her behavior over the last few months, but to no avail. She felt that it was only best for her to nudge away the entire nuisance that had been going on in her mind and move ahead. Yet, a thought lingered in her head the entire night, did she miss something in her life at this point?

The following morning, Jennifer decided to finish off the job no matter what it took. She stretched expansively and placed her feet on the cool floor next to her bed. The first thing she did was to call Zafar. Her eyes kept shutting due to jet lag, but she kept talking to him in a sluggish manner. The clock chimed nine. Zafar had changed the meeting place on her insistence to a site thronged mostly by birds and fringed by parklands. Hauz Khas!

"Thanks, Zafar," Jennifer smiled tiredly. Her hair were disheveled and her socks didn't match. She was wearing her night gown the wrong way. She ordered her regular breakfast of some bread, marmalade, and a hot cup of coffee. She sat in the chair next to her room's window and wondered if coming here was a bad idea. She was astonished that she even did. She sipped her morning coffee in her hotel room quietly and escaped quickly to the new place of meeting. Through the hustle bustle of the city, she eventually reached the place in a cab and walked onwards as Zafar had instructed her. She plugged in her earphones connected to her mobile and walked whimsically through the large assembly of young people. She admired the mystic beauty of the place filled with up-market boutiques, hip bars which were mostly closed, restaurants, and quirky curio shops. She felt peaceful in a way she had never before. The people around her gave her a feeling of great joy. She liked being there, rather than being ensconced in the four walls of a hotel room or a random restaurant. She carefully observed the numerous tombs scattered along the access road to the village as she strolled on until she saw Zafar.

Upon reaching the parkland, she looked at the ruins of the village and saw young people enjoying some unchaperoned time. Zafar was standing at the lakefront by the ruins. He gave her a close-mouthed smile. She walked over to where he stood, wordlessly stealing glances of the people around her.

"Beautiful, isn't it?" Zafar said and leaned in for a handshake when she reached him. He was wearing a tweed jacket over a sweater, jeans, and had paired it with a woollen scarf. In the light of day, she now noticed the crow's feet and the slight greying at his temples, despite his lean and fit figure. His face was set with a light touch of weariness too.

"Ah. Yes. It's beautiful and quiet here, unlike any other place in the city."

"Let's take a walk."

"I'm sorry about yesterday, you know…the way I reacted."

He laughed.

"It would be trite to say what you said yesterday."

"Please. There's a way of complimenting wonderful things, which I seem to have forgotten of late."

"No. But I'm certain you will after this."

"Well, I've been thinking about what you said yesterday."

"What did I say?" Zafar asked.

"Sometimes, all it takes is one incident to change things forever."

"Well, there are too many incidents here."

"I'm curious. I mean, I've heard stories of all sorts from people I've met so far, so I am feeling curious now." Jennifer was unsure whether what she said was in fact true or if she was lying to herself and Zafar.

"Peter told me that you fought with him for this interview."

"Actually, I was against coming here."

"Is that true?"

Jennifer felt embarrassed at the fact that Peter had told him such things.

"My grandfather used to live here. I have an Indian connection in a way."

"But you grew up in London?"

She shrugged.

"I hadn't pegged you as the protesting type," Zafar said, lighting a cigarette.

"I'm usually not. This time, it was due to guilt."

"Guilt?"

"In some way..."

Jennifer chided herself for not wording it better. She had a delicate way of making communication with new people, but this had been in great contrast to her true nature. In order to avoid further questions from Zafar, she asked, "What happened next in your story with our author?"

They kept walking slowly.

"It was the start of autumn and Shimla looked more serene than the preceding years…"

Chapter 3

Seven years ago

It had been raining in Shimla for five hours straight. Amman was waiting in his hotel room for the rain to halt for a while so he could wander outside a little. He had expected to spend his time on the terrace with an unbeatable view of the mountains, as suggested by the hotel staff. He cursed his fate for having missed all the sights on the first day of his arrival. He kept staring out of the window, wistfully admiring the scenic beauty of the place. The raindrops falling on a tarpaulin cover close-by created a symphony so mellifluent to his ears that his incapability to go outside didn't annoy him much after a moment. He knew he had a month to explore each part of this panoramic capital and that he could manage all his explorations in it. All that he hoped was for the rain to stop.

After months of exploring the wild mountains in the heat that the north-eastern states of India experienced, he had been praying for a cooler, chilled out destination. His publishing house had finally granted him his wish and he felt really happy that with little persuasion, everything had worked out in his favor. He made sure that besides his work, he'd find ample time for himself. It was his foremost priority. When the rain subdued to a light drizzle in the evening, he stepped out of the hotel for a leisurely walk with a raincoat on him. He had seen these mountains before and was familiar with the life that people lived in these regions, so there was nothing new that really amused him, besides the fact that he loved those mountains. While walking up to the ridge about which he had heard wonderful things, he remembered Zafar and pulled out his visiting card from his wallet, one that Zafar had given him back in in Darjeeling. He asked a local where he could find the restaurant named *Ashiana*. Upon reaching the ridge, he started capturing the beauty of the mountains, the locals, and their shops in his digital camera. The people there stared at him, as any new entry to their sleepy old commune was a thing of amusement. Someone yelled at him, "Hey, don't take pictures here."

"Don't worry, these are for a magazine," he responded with a casual smile, "I mean no offence." He kept walking and put his camera in his bag. When he reached the top of the ridge, he noticed many other people there, most of them tourists. He walked past the famous Christ Church dominated by the presence of visitors clicking pictures. He glanced at the historic buildings there that included the Town Hall and the Gordon Castle. He fell in love with the place instantly. It didn't come as a surprise to him, for he knew his love for all new places that he visited. This feeling only served as the icing on the cake of a long list of places he had already traveled to.

When he reached *Ashiana*, a fancy restaurant built in a circular shape over the ridge, his eyes searched for Zafar. A pat on his shoulder made him turn and his eyes met Zafar's.

"What a great fortune to see you here!" Zafar exclaimed ecstatically on seeing Amman. Amman graciously gave him a hug which left Zafar astonished as he had not expected this open gesture from him.

"The pleasure is all mine. This is the first place I'm visiting in Shimla."

"I guess it's your first day here then."

"Yes, it is, and what a welcome I've received in your town," Amman gestured towards the glass windows.

"You mean the weather? Oh, it's beautiful, isn't it?

"The nicest I've seen in months..."

Zafar grabbed his hand and took him to a nearby table.

"If I am to be really honest, I should tell you that I didn't expect to see you here so soon. You know, after that brief meeting in Darjeeling, I had not expected you to actually come visit me. You don't expect people to keep their promises these days, especially those made to a stranger. But you didn't disappoint."

Amman nodded and said, "Promises are meant to be kept, it does not matter to whom they are made."

"That's why I'm so happy to see you here," Zafar said. He gestured to one of the attendants and asked for two cups of tea. Amman looked out the windows where it had started to pour down again.

"Does Shimla always have unexpected rains in this season, or is it only because I'm here now?" They shared a laugh at Amman's comment.

"Not always. I'm sure it means something now that you're here," Zafar said, "And I'm sure you must be here for some assignment?"

"Strictly speaking, it is not an assignment. My job isn't as boring as it may sound to some..."

"Of course, not," Zafar said immediately, "Who dislikes traveling? I didn't mean that. Boring, of course not," he said more firmly and laughed it off. "And I insist that you stay here a week more than what you've scheduled."

"I'm pretty sure I'll find enough reasons myself, that you won't have to insist or persuade me to stay here longer," Amman reassured him, as he had already begun to feel a deep connection with the place. It didn't really matter to him if anyone asked him to extend his visit, since he had already decided that he would stretch the duration of his stay there.

He and Zafar were immersed in an amusing conversation about one of the journeys he had taken in the past, when his gaze were attracted all of a sudden by a frail figure that appeared in the gusty rain outside. Half soaked, her dripping hair clung to her face and shoulders. Her face was not clearly visible from the distance. She was dressed casually – a tee and harem pants, with a sling bag over her shoulder. Crouching against the wind and rain, she hastily walked into the restaurant. For a moment or so, Amman's gaze was stuck on her, apparently taken by her beauty. He looked at Zafar in between, but his gaze repeatedly returned to examine her slender figure, enhanced further by the wet clothes she was in. Amman couldn't take his eyes off her. She sneezed. Twice. Amman kept his eyes fixed on her for few more seconds without uttering anything. Zafar was patiently watching him. He noticed how he was looking at her from the moment she had entered the restaurant. He smiled gently.

She choose a table nearby and combed her hand through her hair, trying to untangle the wet knots. She then flipped them back with a single swiping movement of her head.

"Are you ever going to stop looking at her this way?" Zafar asked, trying to break the silence between them. He smiled as Amman glanced back at him.

"She's so beautiful. I've never seen someone like her!" Amman looked at her again. He was awestruck by her glowing beauty and for the first time in his life, he felt short of words.

"You look amused. I guess you are not able to move your gaze away from her," Zafar teased Amman a little, but he couldn't care less. "Go and talk to her."

Amman quickly moved his attention back to him, curious to know if Zafar could help him. "Do you know this girl?"

"She visits here frequently, but always keeps to herself." Zafar looked at her momentarily as he said this. "She seems to be a nice girl."

"What's her name?" Amman asked.

By then, Zafar had understood that Amman really wanted to get to know this girl and that he would have to try to get him acquainted with her.

"Never bothered to ask her. Maybe you could figure out, huh?"

Sure, he did want to know. He continued to look at her obscurely. She had ordered coffee for herself and kept staring outside for a few minutes before taking out a book from her bag. Without meeting anyone's gaze around her, she started to read.

Amman kept an eye on her for as long as he was there, but did not make a move. It felt inappropriate and cliche to just go upto her in a restaurant, although one thing was for sure–he wanted to get to know her anyhow.

When the rain stopped and the clouds dispersed, he left the restaurant and started walking towards his hotel which was almost half an hour away. He walked under the clear moon-lit sky with stars strewn all over it. The roads looked desolate with only a handful of people here and there. Mountain life was a lot different from the city life that he knew. People didn't linger around after dusk here. All shops, barring only a few, had shut already. After minutes of jog-trotting, he managed to cross the ridge and was now merrily humming a song.

It was at this moment that he saw the girl again, passing by him on her cycle. It took only a moment for him to recognize her as she quickly sped by and vanished from his view the very next moment. His heartbeat raced fast in a manner that he had never felt before. He had never had the desire to get to know someone just by how they looked, but this was different from all the girls that he had previously been fascinated by. She seemed to him as a gust of wind that gives a sudden burst of joy, and he didn't mind it. The curiosity to know her that had crept inside him over the last few hours only increased with time. He felt that it was only a matter of time before he would finally lose his heart to her. He wished to never see her again, for he knew what it would do to him.

Ironically, his wish didn't last for even five minutes as he crossed paths with her again and laughed at his fate the moment he saw her. He sighed. When he neared her, he found her fixing the chain of her bicycle. He walked slowly and observed her carefully. He felt it would be foolishness if he let go of the opportunity to talk to her this time. Who knew if he'd be able to see her in these mountains again?

"May I help you?" he asked gently.

She turned to look at him and politely declined the offer.

"It's okay…I don't mean to intrude," saying this, he offered his help again, but received the same answer in return.

"I said, I don't need help. I'll manage on my own. Thank you," she responded sternly and looked askance at him. She then got busy aligning the chain of her bike again. Amman waited for a second, then uttered, "All right. Very well!" and started walking away, though feeling a little disappointed at her apparent arrogance. The girl looked at him obscurely. When she saw him walking away, she regretted being rigid with him for no reason and shook her head.

A few minutes later, she spotted him again at some distance down the hill, whimsically going his way. She felt like she owed him an apology, so she slowly bicycled towards him and called out, "Hey….hey, you! Hi!"

He looked around to find her with a reluctant smile on her face and with no idea as to how he would react.

"Hey…" he uttered, surprised.

"Listen, I'm sorry. I was a little rude before. I didn't mean it."

Amman hardly cared for the apology. He kept looking at her, unable to hide his ecstasy. He failed to comprehend the situation fully and understand why he felt so happy. Was it because of her mesmerising beauty, or that she had come to speak to him? He didn't know. Her eyes looked pale blue even in the dusk and her face had a warm expression on it, clearly wanting to make up for the way she had behaved before. Her skin shone effulgently, perfectly in fusion with the cold weather surrounding them. Her hair were tied in a bun this time. Her apology had altered his perception of her.

"I didn't mean to pry there," Amman said.

"It wasn't your fault. I have had a bad day, plus the evening rain…it all just made things worse for me. I'm really sorry for my behavior back there."

"It's completely fine. You don't have to feel sorry. Any girl would have said the same," Amman replied, trying to lighten the tenor of their conversation.

"The same?" she asked with a smile pressed on her face.

"You know, a strange guy emerging out of nowhere and offering to help fix your bike. I'm sure it might have given you a wrong impression, but honestly, I didn't mean it that way," he explained and wondered why he was saying all that, when he actually wanted to get to know more about her. He tried hard not to stare at her continuously, but his eyes betrayed him and he failed to look away. For a moment, he waited patiently for her to speak and break the awkward silence growing between them, but she didn't and simply kept looking at him as if he had said something displeasing. To avoid any further awkwardness, he began to walk away saying, "I'm sorry. I don't know what I'm saying…"

He could not comprehend the situation he was in and thought of walking away for the best. To his astonishment, however, he heard her calling from behind, "Hey…"

He turned to see her again.

"Who are you?" she asked.

"Look, I'm sorry if you felt otherwise, okay? I didn't mean…"

"You look new here. I have never seen you in this area before. Tourist?" She drew closer to him.

"Sure, you can't possibly know everyone around here, do you?" Amman said. He sensed his despair withering away as she had initiated the conversation this time.

"People here don't just offer help like this."

"You need not belong to a particular place to offer someone help there. Help is help," Amman said. The more he spoke to her, the more relaxed he felt. The enchantment that she held over him made him forget his own existence and presence in that moment. She gave him the feeling of being lost in a strange world.

"So, who's this guy who offers help to strangers? What's his name?" she asked mildly and began to walk ahead with her bicycle. Amman kept looking at her, standing where he was. She turned around and asked, "What?"

Amman shook his head.

"Let's take a walk down the road, if you don't mind."

Of course he didn't mind, but this was beyond his expectations.

"I'm staying at a hotel nearby," he said. They began to walk down the hill, next to each other. "Amman. I'm a traveler."

"So, what's your journey like, Amman? Do you always travel or are you on a vacation or something?" she asked.

"Ah…I'm actually a travel-writer by profession. I'm on one of my assignments here," Amman said.

"You are?"

"Yeah. This is my first visit to your town."

"How cool is that! You must have traveled a lot, to unknown places for days at end…it must be exciting, isn't it?" She spoke rapidly and seemed visibly excited.

Amman nodded and smiled.

"What all have you seen here so far?" she asked, looking pleased now.

"Actually, it's my first day today and thanks to the lovely weather, I could only manage to scale these hills and visit a friend up there…"

"Oh, you already have a friend here…"

"Not really. That restaurant you're coming from, I know its owner."

She stopped abruptly.

"Did you see me there?" she asked, surprised.

"You looked a complete mess." He motioned his hand from her head to toe and giggled.

She started to walk again, Amman followed.

"How long are you here for, Amman?"

"A month."

Judging by the way she interacted with him, Amman could sense that she was more than comfortable in his company, and he couldn't have asked for more. He was simply thrilled to be with her. Now that they were at ease with each other, he felt ecstatic at his decision of having come to this place. They kept talking all the way to Amman's hotel.

"Well, that's where I'm staying," he gestured towards the hotel from a distance. "And you should be hurrying now. It's gotten too late for you."

She smiled. "All right then, I hope…"

"Hey, I didn't get your name…" he interrupted.

"You never asked."

He shrugged and smiled.

"Ayesha."

"I hope to see you soon then, Ayesha."

She nodded. "Yeah. I hope to see you again!"

"Yeah?"

She smiled and gave a nod.

"Good night, Amman."

He was joyous. "Good night."

And Ayesha bicycled her way off in the dark silence.

CHAPTER 4

Amman could not make himself believe how fast his infatuation had turned into a sort of friendship. He kept trying to nudge the thought away, but his heart didn't let him. Perhaps it was the windy winter morning that had given birth to his new love.

He was served an early morning tea by the hotel staff along with a sandwich slice. He had not planned so far how this journey would go, so he took out the local map from his bag and sat on the windowsill to plan his day. Gazing out of the window, he could experience the pleasant weather and feel the cold air kissing his face. He wondered if he would be able to finish off his assignment in time, considering how unexpectedly the weather changed in a jiffy here. He got ready within an hour, carried his bag over his shoulder and hung a camera around his neck to begin his adventure. He had decided to explore the local markets first, but his fate had something else in store for him. Upon reaching the Christ Church which dominated the top of the ridge, he heard a familiar voice, "I hope you're enjoying here…"

He turned around to find the same girl whom he had gone head over heels for the previous night.

"Didn't know you visited the church at this time," Amman said, unable to suppress the excitement of seeing her again so soon.

"I don't. Just happened to see you here while I was passing by."

She looked radiant in broad daylight, much to Amman's delight. Although, it deterred his resolution to not get carried away by her charm, which seemed even more impossible now.

"Where are you heading today?" she asked.

"I've decided to explore the local areas for a day or two. Since I'm alone this time, this journey might be a little slow and boring," Amman said. Even though he tried to suppress every possible thought or desire of seeing her all the time, somewhere he wished for her to join him on a small escapade. He didn't want to ask her directly if she could show him around or perhaps help him with his work, but he knew how to stifle his desires and words before they would come out.

"Maybe you could join us then," Ayesha suggested.

Amman rolled his eyes at her.

"Some friends and I are leaving for Manali in a day or two… probably the day after tomorrow. You must join us as long as your work doesn't get affected by it…"

Amman didn't say anything for a moment and wondered whether it'd be a good idea to agree to it. He looked at her pale eyes and pink cheeks, and waited before he could make up his mind. What was it if not love for her that kept pulling him towards her? He failed to reason with it.

"What happened?" Ayesha asked. "I'm not insisting, you know. You could still carry on…"

"No, no. That isn't what I'm thinking exactly," Amman said. He knew what he feared.

"Then what?"

"Your friends probably won't fancy this idea…"

She looked closely at him. Amman was fair skinned and had a hard face, angular and sharp. His consistent traveling had given him a lean figure, though his muscles were powerful.

"The day after tomorrow. Early morning!" Ayesha said. "If we make good time together, stay with us."

"What if we don't?"

"You do have your job still, no?"

Of course, I do, he thought. And that was the worst thing in all this; to have to think about work when he could actually have a good time with her.

They exchanged phone numbers then and there. Amman wondered if this was actually happening, that too just a day after meeting her for the first time. But deep inside, he was thrilled. Never in his life had Amman experienced things unfolding so spontaneously in his favour; seeing a girl at a restaurant, losing his heart over her in the same moment, then meeting her in the manner that seemed almost orchestrated to perfection. What intrigued Amman the most about his visit to Shimla was how quickly things were happening and for good too.

"Thank you," Amman muttered.

Ayesha met his gaze. "Don't worry. You'll have a good time with us," she assured him.

Amman nodded with a quiet smile. A dense silence grew between them while they kept looking at each other. Amman wondered for a moment what to say next, at first opting to remain quiet, then said softly, "I'll see you soon then."

She nodded. "Enjoy here, meanwhile," she said and retreated on her path. Amman watched her walking away and a smile danced on his face. He couldn't comprehend the series of events happening around him, nor did he try anymore. Not seeking absolute sense out of everything felt more meaningful to him now. He grinned at the thought.

*****

Amman had never been to Shimla before. All that he knew about Shimla came from stories that his father had told him. He had visited other hilly areas on assignments, but this town had long been due for a visit. And certainly, nothing that his father had said could have prepared him for the real hustle-bustle of this town. Everywhere he looked, he saw tourists, overpowering the locals by their sheer number, thronging small cafés and restaurants, and the glass-fronted hotels with bright multi-colored signs. The town was majorly devoid of vehicles with only a few cars to be seen, but they mostly belonged to tourist. Besides that, a few horse-drawn carts jingled up and down the hills all day. The sidewalks he passed through were crowded by small eateries, food stalls, magazine stands, cloth sellers, and a few cigarette and chewing-gum sellers.

He clicked many pictures of all the local places, Christ Church, Gaiety theatre, the town hall–oddly reminiscent of the mansion in Hammer horror films, the Golden Castle and the Rothney castle. His entire day passed by visiting museums and old buildings, while also admiring the scenic beauty of Shimla, but his heart kept lingering back to the thought of being with Ayesha in those mountains, probably forever. It wasn't what he had exactly imagined for this excursion, but his heart wasn't in this assignment anymore. He couldn't get her out of his mind. It was as if she was with him all the time, yet not with him thoroughly enough still.

He was sitting on a sidewalk bench near a restaurant, sharing some local food with a commoner when he asked him, "Do you like this place?"

"Oh, I haven't seen it thoroughly yet. It's beautiful though," Amman said and the local guy laughed.

"That it is. And you'll see a lot more of it ahead."

He knew that. But of course, not without her.

"Though, I've found the people here to be more beautiful than anywhere else," Amman added, and the two shared a laugh.

"Make sure you visit the Kali-Bari Temple. It's about a kilometre west of the ridge, on the hillside above the mall. You might be able to capture some good photographs of Shimla from there."

What Amman remembered the most from that day was his brief conversation with the local. He had sat with him there for almost an hour. It was both strange and wonderful at the same. Though the mountains always gave him a sense of déjà-vu, it was the madding crowd which he always took great notice of. He had made some great friends on such excursions to various places. Within two days, he began to develop a liking for this place for all the obvious reasons.

At midnight, he stood by the window and looked out into the night. Everything was plunged in darkness and a draft of cold wind was blowing in, whistling through a small crack in the wall in one corner of the room. Outside, he could see small lights flickering far away, curtained now and then by the trifling fog. The night seemed long and starless, much like the overcast sky during daytime when the sun made only brief appearances through the chasms in the clouds. He liked being there, sans the aloofness.

*****

"Oh, I took a long detour yesterday and saw many things," Amman said.

"Good, good," Zafar said with a brief smile. "I'm sure it wasn't a detour when you say it."

"Damn, it wasn't," Amman responded with a charmed smile. "But it was good, very good in fact."

Zafar shrugged. "I'm sure it must have been."

Amman had come to visit Zafar at his restaurant the next day.

"And it's that time of the year when it's very crowded. People actually have to search for hotels for vacant rooms, you know," Zafar said.

Amman nodded knowingly.

"But Shimla is a small place, really. Some say it's progressive, and that may be true. It's true enough, I suppose, but it also falls behind in many aspects."

Amman looked at him and blinked.

"Don't get me wrong," Zafar continued. "I would wholeheartedly support any progressive agenda concerning the city. And God knows, this place could use it. Still, this town is sometimes a little too pleased with itself for my taste."

Amman nodded uncertainly, not knowing where the conversation was headed.

"I've always admired the quietness here myself. I have a great fondness for it."

"It's just the kind of place I'd want to settle in for the rest of my life," Amman said, casting him a glance with a glint in his eyes.

Zafar huffed, slapped both his palms against the arms of his chair in excitement, and asked, "May I ask if you have finally found someone?"

"Well. I've experienced the charm, the beauty of this place, the people here, and the unfathomable grace of the face that I had been looking for all my life, so to speak," Amman said and smiled.

A silence followed.

"You cannot be serious, are you?" Zafar was amazed at what he had just heard from Amman. "It's only been two days here for you and you're saying all this?" He couldn't keep his astonishment in check, which suddenly transformed into laughter.

Amman couldn't control himself either and smiled coyly.

"Who is she?" Zafar asked.

"I think it'd be a little too early to say it since I don't know her all that well yet, but in all possibility, yes, she might be the one."

Zafar looked at Amman, his face brimming with happiness.

"And I'm leaving for Manali early tomorrow morning. Thought I should come and meet you before I leave," Amman said and continued, "I'll be gone for a week or so."

"That's great. Go and have fun. You'd love this place, I'm sure about that. Don't forget to capture the scenic beauty along the way. You'll love it."

Amman nodded.

"I wish you had some company, though. It'd have been…"

"Oh, I have, in fact, got some company. I met some people here and we're all going together." He refrained from divulging the details about the nature of this company that he found.

"So, you've already made friends?" said Zafar and looked at him obliquely. "That's wonderful to hear. You won't be alone ahead."

"Yeah, God willing," Amman said slowly.

Zafar looked at him suspiciously as he sensed something beneath Amman's bashful smile that came on every time he said something. He peppered Amman with questions, while the latter kept staring out the window, deeply lost. Questions that were not necessary to be asked, *Who is she? What is her name? Are you two going in a group?* were asked. Amman evaded most of them though.

"I'm sorry if I come across as prying…" Zafar said at last.

"No, you weren't. It's one of those things where too much said can hit you back."

Zafar only gave a nod in response.

"Her name is Ayesha," Amman eventually confessed.

"It will be good to have company on this journey. A little different, for a change. A little life," Zafar said playfully.

Amman waved a hand and laughed it off.

"But I fear something, Zafar," Amman said, tapping a finger against his cup.

"What?"

"No," he struggled to find words. "I mean..." he grinned to himself when he noticed Zafar staring at him. He then looked away, pretended as if it wasn't worth discussing.

"I hope it doesn't turn out to be one of those stories where you meet someone and then drift apart for nothing."

Amman suspected that Zafar had understood everything by then, what his fear was and what he carried in his heart for Ayesha. But what good would it do, he thought. He stood up and said, "I'll be back by next week."

Chapter 5

Ayesha was a surprise.

Astonished and puzzled, Amman saw her from the window of his hotel room, as if he had not expected to see her. It was five in the morning and everything was quiet and still enveloped in darkness. He hadn't slept properly in the last two nights for the restlessness he had acquired since meeting her. He looked at his watch with pain in his eyes, not noticing the other people in the car behind.

"I'm sorry," Ayesha spoke slowly over call, careful not to disturb the calmness of early dawn. "But we need to leave now. Get yourself ready in ten minutes."

Outside, in the early morning chill, Amman glanced at a local guy who had lit a fire to keep himself warm, then walked away from the window to pack all his belongings. Meanwhile, Ayesha stepped out of the car when she saw the flames taking form and walked closer to it, raising her hands–palms open–towards it. From here, she could see the ridge as well as the Christ Church where she had been going ever since she had come to realise its architectural elegance and the library behind it which was the perfect place for anyone to get lost in a different world entirely. She then gazed up at the morning stars, fading pale, blinking at her indifferently. She sighed to a sense of belonging to that place.

"Ayesha, come inside. It's cold out there," someone from the car said, her voice ringing loud and clear in the still morning.

"You should come out instead, Nina. It's beautiful here."

"We're moving in a few minutes anyway and I'm all tucked in a blanket. Happy watching," said the other guy.

Ayesha smiled briefly and shrugged. "Lazy asses!"

She tried to gather herself and, in a few moments, caught sight of Amman approaching them with a bag over his shoulders and another trolley bag in his hand.

"I thought you'd let me know beforehand that you were coming. I could've gotten…"

"You really don't like surprises, do you?"

"Yes."

"Here we are then, travellers."

He tried to avert his eyes each time she passed by him, but whenever their gazes met by chance, he nodded at her and blood rushed to his face in excitement.

Ayesha helped him keep his luggage in the boot of her car and introduced him to her friends.

"You'll have the company of these two from now on," she said and gestured towards her two friends settled quite comfortably in the back seat of the car. "Guys, this is Amman, our new friend on this journey."

"I hope you guys don't mind," Amman said promptly.

"If we did, you wouldn't have found us here at this time of the day," Nihit said.

Never in his life before had Amman felt so conscious of himself, and he knew it was all because of Ayesha. He didn't miss a chance to steal a glance at her whenever possible.

"Amman, he's Nihit," Ayesha introduced and they both shook hands.

"Yeah, but call me Jerry," interrupted Nihit.

"He doesn't like his own name; feels it's too difficult for others to pronounce."

"Besides the fact that I don't like this name myself. Simple as that," he concluded.

"And she's Nina, the darling of my eye," said Ayesha, gesturing at the girl next to him.

Nina extended her hand to shake Amman's. "Don't worry, it isn't any trouble. We'll have a good time, I'm sure," said Nina cheerfully and smiled at Amman.

"Have you been to Shimla before?" asked Nihit.

"Come on, get inside first. We have the rest of the way for this conversation," Ayesha said and nudged Amman to take the front seat next to her. The air inside the car felt thick with the smell of perfume and something else that Amman didn't recognize; something sweet and strange.

"Ayesha mentioned that you're a travel writer and are here for some work…" Nina said.

"It's my first visit here, that too for an assignment," Amman replied.

"How could you miss this place being a traveler, huh?" Nina asked. She sat in the back, her legs crossed over the seat, all cozied up in a blanket, while Nihit was seated next to her in the same manner.

"Yeah well, we are assigned our locations. This is something beyond our control," Amman said.

"Lucky you! We remain in these mountains all our life," Nihit retorted.

"See, that's the fun everybody misses…" said Amman.

Nihit shook his head and looked away.

"But tell us Amman, how long are you staying here for?" Nina asked.

Amman looked at Nina and uttered, "Would forever be too long to say?"

Ayesha looked at Amman and sensed something alarming in his tone, but cared not to let it appear on her face. Nina slumped back in her seat with a sigh, hugging her blanket the way a pregnant woman might hold her protruding belly. "Gosh, this fascination!"

"But it's beautiful here, isn't it?" Amman said.

"Say that to someone who's oblivious to the beauty of this valley," Nina said, patting Amman's shoulder.

"You haven't seen half the charm of it yet," Ayesha said.

"And she isn't exaggerating," Nina said, casting Amman a warm glance.

"That I'm quite sure about."

As he grew more comfortable in their company, he shared with them stories of his escapades to various places along his journey. He told them how he threw away a career in newspaper journalism and hit the road as a travel writer a few years ago, not long after realizing that good food, good music and the awesome experience called life existed outside the confines of a sanitized office cubicle. While on his assignments, he had traced the seldom travelled routes across east and north-east India, meditating in Bodhgaya, befriending the rhinos in Kaziranga's grasslands, quaffing *chhang* (barley beer) with Sikkimese villagers, trundling through Arunachal's primordial forests, gorging on Nagaland's porky delights, grooving to the blues in Meghalaya and feasting his eyes on southern Bengal's gold & green rice fields.

"What is it like, travelling to all these places?" Nina asked.

"What is it like? I think it's life which you never get to see sitting inside office cubicles. Had I not left that work, I would never have experienced all these adventures."

Earlier, Amman had tried to stay calm in appearance, but he was frantic inside, as he always felt around Ayesha. As he started to narrate those experiences however, he gained more confidence and did not shy away from letting anything out.

"And what has been the funniest incident of them all?" Nina asked. Of the three, she seemed to be most interested in hearing those tales.

"There have been many, if I tell you. I remember one genuinely scary road chase where I had some crazy hotel touts after me, but I was saved by a guardian angel with a fast moped. A man once threw up all over me in a packed bus, and once I was nearly attacked by a monkey."

"That's hilarious, Amman," Nina said as they all laughed at his funny anecdotes.

While narrating those incidents, Amman chanced a quick glance at Ayesha now and then and found, to his great relief, the corners of her mouth curled up in a shadow of a smile. Of all the four, however, it was Nina who did most of the talking. Wrapped up in a blanket in the back seat, Nihit soon fell asleep. Ayesha joined the two in between. Amman's tales of his adventures kept the mood alive and light throughout the way. Nina would laugh aloud at the very mention of something funny from Amman, while Ayesha mostly just smiled. She didn't speak much while driving, but once she was on the road in daylight, she started to converse actively too.

"So, tell us some more funny incidents from your journeys, Amman. Something you cherish…tell us."

It was late morning by then and Nihit had woken up too.

"I thought everything I said was funny, no?" Amman said and grinned. He heard a low chuckle from the backseat.

"Of course, Amman. It's just hard to make Ayesha laugh at times," said Nina.

"Well, there isn't much else to say in that sense. They're like any other incidents."

Oh, surely. But there must be something which amazed even you," Ayesha said.

He kept quiet for a moment, recollecting his memories and wondering himself. What could he possibly say that might capture

Ayesha's fancy? He was desperate too to retrieve something from his past that might be of interest to her or amuse her.

"Well, I was once with these buffalo herders…" No sooner had he uttered these words, he wished to slap his own face. *Buffalo herders?*

"Ahh."

"In Uttarakhand, I travelled with the nomadic water buffalo herders into the Himalayas where I joined some religious worshippers on a mountainous pilgrimage trail."

Ayesha giggled, so did Nina and Nihit in the backseat.

"You actually crossed the state with nomads on your way to the Himalayas? That too with buffalo herders?" Ayesha looked at him and asked.

"With some tribal villagers too…precisely," Amman concluded.

Ayesha suddenly burst out laughing, but it only added to her already enormous allure and mystery. Her laughter rang in his ears for a long time that day. To Amman, it was a great relief. Heartened now, he heard himself say, "May I tell you another story?"

"By all means…" said Nina excitedly.

Amman didn't think of himself as a very good storyteller, if not on paper, but he could not escape the charm and mystery that surrounded Ayesha. He wanted to know more about her, see her laugh, or even smile coyly. He found himself talking more and more for her sake and realized that it suited him. He was happy to unlid the Pandora's box of stories from his multitude of adventures. When he got tired after a while, he kept mum, but the mood was kept alive by stories mutually shared. Ayesha talked minimally all the while. Five hours after starting their journey, they stopped at a local restaurant alongside the road to have breakfast.

"Are you fine, Jerry?" Amman asked Nihit as he stepped out of the car with a hand over his belly.

"He has no sense of fun or adventure," Nina said. "He's boring, I tell you…"

"What happened to you? You don't look good, Jerry," Ayesha walked up to him and held his hand. "What happened?"

"I've had this stomach ache since morning. I thought it'd get fine with time, but I guess it didn't."

"And you're telling us now, stupid," Nina said in anger.

"Nina!" Ayesha looked at her with narrowed eyes.

Amman helped Nihit into the restaurant and made him sit.

"Do you need something?" Ayesha asked. "Tea? Coffee… anything?"

"No. It will make it worse. I just need to be here for some time. I'll be fine, I hope," Nihit said in pain.

"Have a cup of tea or something. You'll be fine."

"Oh no, please," Nihit said, resting against the wall. "You guys get something. I'll just rest here for a while."

Nina looked at him and shrugged. They took a table and ordered an assortment of snacks with tea. Nina sat toying with the car keys. Ayesha again asked, "You sure you don't need anything at all?"

"How far from here?" Nihit asked.

"We're still way too far from Manali," Ayesha said.

"Yes, but how far?"

"It will take a day to reach there," Nina said, still fiddling with the keys.

"God," he muttered.

"If you want, we can wait here for a while. There's no hurry," Ayesha said.

"Don't say that you can't even sit inside the car now. All you have to do is just sit and do nothing."

"That's rude, Nina…" Amman said.

"Nina!" Ayesha gave her a grave look.

"What?"

"Let him rest. Please."

"I don't think he wants to continue," Nina said as she watched him close his eyes to rest. "I don't think he will…"

Amman considered what to do for a moment, opting to remain quiet at first, then said, "We'll let him rest here for a day. But what if he doesn't feel good enough to carry on with the rest of the journey?"

Ayesha nodded.

They all had a quiet breakfast. Amman looked out to take in the sight of the plains all around them, white and yellow, withering from one end of the horizon to the other, with sunlight kissing the mountain tops. He looked at the hills and the power poles dispersed intermittently throughout the scenery. His eyes followed after the vehicles zooming past the restaurant and wondered how happily he would spend the rest of his life in those mountains. Forever? Perhaps.

"We'll stay here tonight," Ayesha said at last. "I don't think he'll make it there in this condition. It's best if we just stay here for the rest of the day."

"Yes," Amman said.

They found a hotel nearby and pulled the car over to the side of the road. Ayesha didn't speak for a long time. When Nina and Nihit stepped out of the car, Ayesha said, "Thank you, Amman."

"For what?"

"For being so receptive towards everything. I know you're here for work, and now because of me…"

"It's all fine," Amman interrupted. "I don't mind any of this."

"No, you don't understand," Ayesha said tiredly.

"I think we don't need to. Besides, I don't mind the company of you all. I was alone anyway."

To this, Ayesha had nothing to say.

"Are we all going inside now?" Nina came back and said tiredly.

"Yes," Ayesha cleared her throat and stepped out. Amman remained quiet for a moment, then stepped out after her.

*****

This was not the first time that Amman was randomly meeting new people. He had experienced all this before, so it wasn't something he was not prepared for. But Ayesha had come into his life quite unexpectedly. This wasn't something that any of his past experiences had prepared him for. She was a surprise, like a rainbow after a sudden downpour in daylight. He even considered for a while to leave everyone behind and finish his assignment. But the thought of Ayesha held him back. He had agreed to go on this short excursion with all of them, and leaving them behind would have deterred them all, especially Ayesha. He dropped the idea soon after.

Ayesha and Nina were in different rooms, while Amman and Nihit took adjacent ones. In the evening, Amman saw Ayesha outside the hotel, standing near her car and staring into the distance with a blank expression on her face and a cigarette in her hand. He kept looking at her through the window for a while, then finally made the effort to walk up to her.

"Are you fine?" he asked calmly.

"How's Nihit now?"

"He's recuperating, I guess," Amman said. "He's sleeping."

Amman noticed that Ayesha made no effort to make conversation sometimes. She remained mostly to herself even when surrounded by people. It was a little mysterious, to put it in a subtle manner. Or at least, it created an air of mystery around her.

"Do you always stay quiet like this?" he could not stop himself from asking after a certain point.

"What's your next destination after Shimla?" Ayesha asked.

"Ah. I'm not quite sure of that. Probably Kashmir."

"You're blessed," Ayesha said. "You're doing what you love to do." She smiled at Amman, but he remained expressionless.

"And you?" asked Amman at his desperate best to know her. She kept silent for a while, puffing out clouds of smoke every few seconds, intensifying the air of something hidden or unintelligible around her persona. Amman could only wonder.

"I'm a bird. I don't wish to stay in one place for long. And Shimla? It cannot be my destiny." She looked at Amman with eyes that he could only hope to fathom. He knew that there was something obscure, some sort of distinctiveness about them.

She lit another cigarette.

"But Shimla is your home, no? Where do you wish to go from here?" he asked.

She sighed. "Well, some other time," she said.

Amman cast a skeptical glance at her. The more closely he looked at her, the more strikingly attractive she seemed to him, being at the peak of her beauty with that smooth flawless skin and flirtatious eyes. Although she didn't speak much, there was something about her demeanor that revealed her intelligence. Under her penetrative gaze, anyone could feel appraised or charmed. Amman could not escape from all this and Ayesha noticed how he looked at her.

"When people reveal too much, they destroy the essence of everything."

"I'm curious why you say this…"

"If you'll know too much about me, you'll get bored," she said and took another puff.

They shared a brief grin.

"If I tell you too much about who I am, there will be nothing left to assume or perceive. I'll be another passing fancy from one of the journeys that you'll be on. I'd rather have you wonder about me more," she said in a confidential tone.

"And what makes you believe that?"

"Because I know you will," she smiled and offered him the cigarette.

"No," Amman said.

"I'm impressed."

"I don't think so," he said.

"Why not?"

"You look like you're dying to be rescued."

Ayesha laughed at this. "Do I?" she asked.

"Only that you're scaring me now…"

She smiled momentarily and none spoke for a few minutes, silently looking at the mountains surrounding them. A momentary silence was fine, but a silence that stretched for that long always bothered Amman. He stole glances at her in between. The way she stood made her seem like some actress from an old silent film.

"It seems like you are dying to be rescued right now," Ayesha joked.

"Are you leaving now?"

"Do you want me to stay?"

"Yes."

"Then I'll stay."

Amman was grateful for that, although he could not find the exact reason why he felt that way. There was some sort of kindness that he felt towards her, without even knowing her thoroughly enough.

"Don't worry. You'll be alright."

"Ah, yes. You know, I'm a little frightened of you…"

"We all are."

Amman smiled, embarrassed. “You don’t seem to be frightened though.”

“I told you, if I tell you too much about me…you’ll be disappointed.” As always, Ayesha tried to mask her vulnerability and nervousness every time someone complimented her, especially men.

“How old are you?” Amman asked without any reluctance.

She looked at him, not able to comprehend the intent behind such a question.

“Your words seem way beyond your age, you know,” Amman said further.

“Please. This is getting too obvious now. And I tell you, there is an art to complimenting a woman. Age?” she chuckled.

“I’m not good at it. I’m sorry.”

They shared a brief laugh.

Later, amidst a general conversation about stories from his past, Amman revealed how much he wanted to travel all around the world, and the one place in particular.

“Where?”

“Paris.”

“I want to travel too,” Ayesha said. “I’ve always wanted to travel. To no specific place, no destination…but to just wander.”

“Like a nomad?”

“They say, not all those who wander are lost. Are you?”

He took a moment before he uttered with a casual smile, “Well, I’ve been thinking about it. I mean, this is what I love to do, but I’ve never put a label on my profession.”

“You see what I’m saying. No specific place, no destination… just me wandering.”

Amman smiled. “I didn’t ask you what you do exactly…” he started.

"I've ruined your journey with all this," Ayesha said, while her hand motioned towards the hotel. "I'm sure it wasn't meant to go like this," she muttered.

"Things happen. Besides, I don't mind a change from the regular excursions that I go on."

Ayesha smiled tiredly.

"And you always manage to evade these normal conversations."

"You hardly know me…"

Amman sighed and looked away. "Such mystery, huh?"

"You're very impulsive."

"Yeah, whatever!"

Amman began to walk away and Ayesha noticed a shadow of disappointment on his face. It suddenly struck her how easily she could disappoint people around her.

"I used to write. Once."

Amman stopped on hearing her words.

"During college. I mean, I love to write," she said, feeling guilt now.

"I'm sure you write very well then."

She told him how she found comfort in writing and not knowing absolutely everything was something that she enjoyed.

"I wrote a book once. Well, not exactly a book…more like a collections of poems."

"Did you get it published?"

"I don't write for anyone. It never crossed my mind…getting published."

"I'm curious. I mean, I'd like to see some of those."

She laughed and said, "They aren't as great as you might think."

"I'm not assuming them to be great," replied Amman. "But yes, I'd like to read them."

Ayesha was inwardly flattered. She had never told anyone about her writing before, not even Nina. Then, why Amman? She observed that whatever she said, Amman listened in a way that none ever had before. She could see his interest for her writing as he talked about it more and more, perhaps a little mystified by her passion for it. He made light-hearted jokes, but did not make fun of it. She chuckled and enjoyed whatever he said.

"The work that I do is frivolous..." Ayesha said.

"It's not frivolous if you find comfort in it. You're not writing to be judged by anyone for it. It's just you."

She nodded.

Amman asked her more about her poems and she spoke about them without any hesitation now. She knew that she would not be judged on it, and that Amman would not form opinions about her based on this. She grew more comfortable as she talked, but soon changed the subject. She didn't want to continue talking about herself for too long.

"Who all are in your family, Ayesha?"

She shut her eyes and said immediately, "We should go for dinner now."

"What?" Amman asked, taken aback. But Ayesha had already walked away.

*****

Ayesha walked into Nihit's room. His hair were disheveled and he smiled tiredly at her.

"How bad is it?" she asked.

Ayesha noticed that Nihit had wrapped himself up in two quilts. A glass of water and a few medicines were kept on his bed-side table.

"I've ruined your journey, Ayesha. I'm sorry," Nihit muttered.

"It's nothing. Stop thinking about it."

"I feel I can sleep here for weeks," he laughed.

"Will you be alright?"

"Not anytime soon, I think," he said.

By that time, Nina had also walked into the room. "We should take him back, I guess," she said.

"No. No one has to come with me. I'll be fine. Just need to get back home. I will be fine there." His eyes drifted shut, though he kept talking in a sluggish manner.

"Do you want to eat something?" Ayesha asked.

"No, I feel okay this way. Food will only deteriorate my health at this time."

Both Ayesha and Nina kept looking at him quietly. Nihit cracked open an eye halfway.

"Chill, guys, I'm okay right now. Get something to eat for yourself. Where's Amman? Is he roaming around alone out there?" he changed the subject, not wanting to talk about his health the entire time.

For dinner, everyone collected in Nihit's room. Ayesha told Amman that Nihit had a stone in his kidney which was causing him so much pain and trouble. She told him how the same thing had occurred with him for the first time about three years ago while they were at a restaurant. Unable to endure the agony, he had pressed his knees into his stomach. While he was barely able to hold on to his consciousness, the people around him could not figure out what had happened to him. When the staff at the restaurant finally took him to a hospital nearby, it was revealed that the problem was kidney stones.

"You should get it removed then," Amman said while taking a sip of his coffee.

"I will. I will. I'll leave tomorrow and get it fixed," Nihit said and laughed.

"What…you're leaving?" Amman asked, shocked.

Nihit nodded smiling.

"It's necessary," Nina said.

"You guys must carry on with your journey. I will take a bus and will be home in a few hours."

"That's easy for you to say, but no. We'll come along," Nina said.

"Shut up, Nina…"

"And what if it starts hurting on the way? Don't be absurd."

"And you all will be able to lessen the pain then?"

"Of course not. But there's got to be someone with you." Amman didn't know much about his health, but he knew that he couldn't let him go alone.

"Of course."

Ayesha was standing by the window. Nihit looked at her and laughed.

"You hear that…" he said.

Ayesha smiled. "They're all right in what they're saying."

"Yeah, probably, but I can't let you guys screw up your journey just because of me. And Amman is here for the first time. I don't want him to take away such trivial memories from Shimla due to us stupid jerks. Don't spoil his brief sojourn. Please!"

"Your friend looks angry," Amman said while looking at Ayesha and laughed.

"I'm not. This would be a matter of great guilt for me if you guys screw this up because of me."

"Guilt?"

"Yes."

Amman laughed again.

"Okay. Drop it now. I'll accompany you back home. How about that?" Nina said at the end. "Nobody has to end anything. Ayesha and Amman can go on from here. I'll come with you. Someone's got to be with you. I'll sacrifice for now." Nina cried animatedly, making everyone laugh.

"Do as you like," Nihit said and turned his face away.

"So, it's decided now," Nina said as if she had won a battle.

When Nina told Ayesha and Amman about the places in Shimla to visit and how to reach them, Amman noticed something very innocent in her nature. He understood it in a way that Nihit couldn't, something that she had never openly admitted to anyone.

"Will you come with me?" Amman asked Ayesha.

"It was I who invited you to come with us. I can't just leave you here now."

"No. I could still go…"

"Shut up," Nina interrupted. "I'm not making all these shitty plans for you to go on alone."

Amman raised both his hands and bowed down to Nina in a gesture of submission.

Nina made sure that everyone was convinced with what she had in her mind. Both Nihit and Ayesha knew by then that she was not going to listen to them anymore, so they gave in to her demands.

Chapter 6

The next morning, Nina and Nihit took a bus back to Shimla.

"I'm going to call you," Ayesha said to both when they were leaving.

"I know. I know," Nihit said. "Although, you don't need to worry."

"Ah sorry, Amman. It didn't go as we had planned. But I hope to see you back in Shimla," Nina said and gave him a hug. She whispered to him slowly, "I think she's going to be fine with you."

Amman looked at her, but could not decipher what that had meant. Nina just blinked with a smile.

The sun had risen and so had the people. Having been to the mountains before, Amman knew that people in these regions woke up at early dawn. All around him, beyond the bright sunlight, was the endless desolate expanse of mountains swallowed up by the solitariness. That's how Amman always felt every time he was in the mountains.

"If you wait until dusk, you'll lose the beauty," Ayesha said.

"I'm already losing it."

She smiled.

"Let's just go," Ayesha said clearing her throat, and lifted her face up to the bright sky. "And this weather…"

Amman looked at her.

"I want to smoke now."

Amman began to protest, but stopped himself. "Why do you smoke so much?" he asked calmly.

"If you don't, how would you know?"

"I tried once…didn't work for me," he said and smiled.

Ayesha stood motionless for a long time, while Amman turned to walk away.

Have heart, he almost heard himself saying to Ayesha.

"I'll be right back." She looked down and shuffled her feet for a moment.

"Oh yes," Amman said, "That's okay."

He walked back to the hotel to take a shower and got ready within half an hour. He took a quick glance around outside the window. A few minutes later, he found himself knocking on Ayesha's door, and saw for the first time what she'd be like if she were an ordinary person. Although she was one, Amman had always seen her in a different light before. She was wearing jeans and a red top, and though her hair were still pulled up in a bun, she looked more casual than she usually did. He realized she could actually be cute if she gave herself the opportunity beyond her usual sad face. That's what he observed in her.

"Are we okay?" Amman asked.

"Would you like some lemonade while we sit?" she asked. "I ordered some for myself."

"Well, if that eases the mountain journey, I'd love some," he said.

Amman noticed on Ayesha's bedside table, there was a book– 'Faith Is The Answer'.

"Were you reading last night?"

"I usually do before I sleep."

She quickly put on a shrug over her red top and undid the bun. Taking the chair opposite Amman, she lit a cigarette and took a puff.

"What?" she asked as she noticed how Amman kept his gaze fixed on her. He then leaned forward, took the cigarette from between her lips and threw it away in a bin.

"What are you doing?" Ayesha asked, quite stupefied at what Amman had just done. No one had ever done something like that before, and she had not expected it from him either.

"That's what you want?"

This time, Ayesha didn't respond. They sat in silence for a few minutes.

A moment later, a server from the hotel knocked on the door and entered with two glasses of lemonade.

"It's a beautiful day," Ayesha finally said with a smile.

"Yes, it is."

"Warm too."

"That's because you're in the sun."

She had a slight smile on her face all this while.

"We should be leaving now," Amman said as he drowned his lemonade.

They checked out from the hotel and moved towards the parking. Ayesha started the car and they took the road leading to Manali.

"How well have you planned your excursion to this place? What places do you intend to visit?" Ayesha asked.

"I'd be happy if you could show me something besides the usual."

Ayesha nodded without saying anything.

"I mean, I have a few places in mind. I'm on a month-long stay here. I hope that'd be enough."

"Not really."

"A month is not long enough?" Amman asked and smiled surprisedly.

"I guess not, sir." Ayesha looked at him and shrugged.

He kept looking at her for a long time, as if thinking about her. "Do you mind if I ask you a question?"

"As long as you don't disappoint me with routine conversation, yes."

Amman was astounded, for it seemed she already knew what he was going to ask her.

"I don't know what you mean…"

"You have to promise that you won't fall in love with me."

Amman knew she was joking from the way she laughed as soon as she had said this. He couldn't help but breathe a sigh of relief. He smiled and gave her his word.

"So tell me, Amman," Ayesha asked, "Where's your family?"

Here we go, Amman thought to himself. "My family…all of a sudden?" he asked, amazed.

"We are going to spend a hell lot of time together. What else do you think are we going to do?" Ayesha looked at him strangely.

"I'm sure you could've asked me something besides this," Amman said, trying his best to play it cool.

"Don't worry, we have a lot to talk about," Ayesha said, and even though they both knew that it was true, the conversation had to begin somehow and with something.

"My mother lives in Mumbai. She's a teacher at a college there."

"And your father?"

"He lives in London. We don't talk much."

"Are they separated?"

"That's how it seems to me, at least. They're not divorced though."

Ayesha didn't say much while he spoke about his family, although she was the one who had asked him about it in the first place.

"That's one reason why I refrain from talking about my family," he said. "I've grown pretty much without a father in my life. He used to visit us sometimes back when I was studying, but we rarely talked even then. I don't know why."

"What about your mother? Does she talk to him often?" Ayesha asked reluctantly.

"I have never seen her; not in front of me, I guess."

Amman looked out of the car's window without any intent of nudging the thought away. He wondered why his parents never got divorced. He had grown up under his mother's care and she had given him the best she could, that he knew well. However, he had missed a strong male influence in his life. It did not make him hard, or rebellious, but the thought annoyed him sometimes.

"Do you miss your father?" Ayesha asked as she steered through the narrow hilly roads.

"I hardly lived with him. I don't even know what missing someone means."

Ayesha shot a quick glance his way while he stared out of the window.

"I was only five when he left. He never came back to stay for long thereafter," Amman said and smiled. "I don't know what missing someone means," he reiterated.

"Your eyes don't reflect that. You always seem happy. I've seen children who grow up without a parent, either father or mother, and they're always sad in a strange way. Not that they're crying all the time…"

"Of course, not…"

"But they have this rebellious streak in them, that they didn't get what they deserved. You're certainly not one of them."

"How will it help, being rebellious?"

Ayesha kept quiet.

"Talk about something else," Amman said cheerfully.

"Sure."

"You know, I've noticed that you always seem to be trying to unravel some puzzle in your mind. You wish to laugh out like a mad woman, but you hold yourself back. Why is that?"

Ayesha turned to face him as if someone about to reveal one's deepest secret in public. She was surprised, but tried not to let it show on her face.

"You can tell me if there's something that bothers you inside. I hardly know you, and I have nobody else to reveal it to. This will only be between us. Only with me rather," Amman insisted.

He observed that Ayesha wasn't someone who wore makeup all the time. In fact, not once had he noticed any of it on her face. A look of confusion crossed Ayesha's face, as though she was trying to put together another complicated puzzle.

Amman kept waiting patiently. He felt sure by then that there was indeed something that bothered Ayesha, but it wasn't perhaps the best time to talk about it.

"Ayesha?"

She didn't utter a word, but simply kept driving while Amman kept looking at her.

"Are you staring at me?" Ayesha asked all of a sudden.

"Yes."

"Be careful. I told you something," she said and smiled.

"And you're only pushing this further into my mind, although I can't stop myself from feeling so."

Her eyes narrowed. "Well…"

Amman looked out of the window again. He didn't expect to hear anything from Ayesha soon. He started humming a song, being his usual best–a little whimsical. His lips barely moved as he hummed under his breath, a rhythm he always resorted to when there was nothing left to say, or to expect in return. Amman was a person who couldn't wait for the murkiness to clear. He preferred being true to his casual self.

"Amman? What is that?" Ayesha asked.

"What?"

"That song you are singing–what is it?"

"It's like a nursery rhyme, rather a lullaby," Amman said. "My mother used to sing this to me when I was very young. I learned this from her."

Ayesha nodded. "It's beautiful. Please sing it again."

...Smile, though your heart is aching

smile, even though it's breaking

when there are clouds in the sky, you'll get by

if you smile through your fear and sorrow

smile and maybe tomorrow

you see the sun come shining through for you...

Amman noticed that Ayesha was smiling, but had tears welling up her eyes.

"What happened, Ayesha?"

Ayesha stopped the car, lowered her head and shook it slowly.

"Tell me. Please."

She shook her head again. "No. No. It's okay."

Amman reached for Ayesha's hands and took them in his own. Ayesha didn't say anything, but then she grinned with her eyes still moist. She looked at him with eyes that Amman couldn't read into, but knew somewhere that she was in pain.

"You know that you can tell me anything. It's only going to be between you and me anyway."

Ayesha let out a sudden chuckle that sounded more like a deep cry, and she covered her mouth.

"We can move now."

"And these secrets of yours…." Amman shook his head.

"Please don't tell anyone about this," Ayesha said.

"You've hardly told me anything," Amman said and chuckled.

"…about my crying, or I'll kill you."

Amman figured Ayesha could really drive a guy crazy sometimes.

"It's okay," Amman shrugged, doing his best to play it cool again.

Ayesha elbowed him in the ribs playfully and he grunted.

"You're impossible."

"Now, come on. Drive the car."

Amman had realized by that time that they both were treading on dangerous ground. He wasn't sure about how Ayesha felt for him, but he knew these emotional talks and then the *playing it cool* thing was soon going to change for him, if not for her. Amman knew Ayesha was probably the best girl that he had met in his life so far.

When they reached Manali later that evening, Amman decided to explore the local market and the surrounding areas on his own, leaving Ayesha back at the hotel, primarily because he did not want her to be a distraction in what he had come for. He spotted multiple families and couples on honeymoon who had come there to enjoy the cool mountain air and to have their first experience of snow. He had done his own research and knew that he'd see a lot of backpackers who hung out in the hippy villages around the main town or went for trekking, paragliding, rafting and skiing.

When Amman was done with his local exploration and research, he called Ayesha for dinner and waited for her at a small restaurant.

"You must have visited all these places many times before, right?" Amman asked.

"This is more likely to be my home. I've seen all these places numerous times," Ayesha

answered. "I wish to escape these mountains, though."

"Why so?"

"I feel sometimes that I'd remain confined within these mountains all my life. That'd be so boring, no?"

"And where do you plan to leave for?" Amman asked, knitting his eyebrows.

There was a short pause on the other end.

"Ayesha?"

"I don't know. Maybe just travel the world all my life. For nothing."

"For nothing?"

It took Ayesha another few seconds to get more words out.

"Well...people want to travel the world, you know...to explore, meet new people, see new places, but I just want to travel."

"I told you...you're dying to be rescued."

"Not really," Ayesha said, again with her *playing cool* attitude.

"You know, you're not as cool as you pretend to be. And the girl I see in you is definitely not what you put out. You're more than this inside."

Ayesha ignored it and went on, "And where's the food?"

"There's something I want to talk to you about, and I wouldn't ask if it weren't important."

"And what is it?" Ayesha tried to disguise the growing surprise in her voice.

"I think you know what it is..."

With that, Ayesha suddenly realized that Amman wasn't going to let her off the hook easily, and that they'd end up talking one way or the other.

"No," Ayesha said.

"I think it's the right time…"

Amman noticed for the first time that Ayesha actually looked nervous sitting opposite him.

"Well, I don't know," Ayesha said, confused.

But Amman knew that Ayesha wasn't the sort of girl who'd get confused or nervous that easily. She always evaded it every time he tried to talk to her about that unknown thing which intrigued him so much. Whenever he looked at her, he could tell how important it really was for her. The simple fact that she was hiding something–for that's how it seemed to Amman–made it all the more imperative for him to know what it was, so she could open herself up to him. She was caged somewhere. Deep down, he suspected that no one had ever asked her this because of the way she was. He had understood by then that Ayesha wasn't one who could be understood easily. That very realization made him sad.

"So, where do you plan to go after this?" Ayesha asked, stalling his direction of conversation yet again, but Amman realized what she was doing. He didn't mind.

"A vacation…maybe!" Amman said and chuckled.

"You also need a vacation? I thought your work is a vacation itself."

Amman nodded and laughed. "I know, that's how anyone would see it, but traveling is my life. I enjoy doing it."

She nodded.

"I may visit London after this for a week or so."

"And you're so orthodox when it comes to traveling. Why London?"

"What's wrong with that?" Amman asked.

"You should visit some better nicer place. I've studied in London and it can get so boring at times."

"Really? I didn't know that," Amman said with a suppressed surprise in his voice.

"What? That I studied in London, or that it's boring…?"

"Actually, both."

Ayesha kept smiling while Amman took a large swig from his Budweiser can.

"I thought you'd rather visit some unexplored place. London isn't always beautiful. Not if you go there for a vacation, at least."

Amman wiped his lips with the back of his hand.

"Maybe you could suggest someplace to me."

"No."

"Why not?"

"I'm sure you'll find some nice place on your own. London is so not you."

Amman immediately smiled to himself. "Now that's funny..."

Ayesha looked at him and wondered what he meant. "Why so?"

"Because you already know me, so much so that you could go on to say that London is not my kind of a place."

"Well, I could figure out that you're not that sort of a person."

"Oh…I see," Amman said, trailing off. He paused again before saying, "You figure out everything about others, but keep yourself within a closed loop. I'm here with you and still don't know much about you besides that you've studied in London and that you're from Shimla."

It took Ayesha another few seconds to respond, "Is it really necessary to know more?"

"What's the harm in it?"

Amman could tell that this held some significance for her. She was hiding something that hurt her deep down too.

"Maybe I should leave it for now. This persistence isn't too good to last for this long," Amman said finally.

"You give up very easily, Amman," Ayesha said softly.

"I really don't have a choice now, do I?"

Ayesha straightened up a little in her seat and looked at him sadly, aware that he was disappointed now. She knew how Amman felt, how she usually made others feel like this.

Amman found himself running out of things to say after that. A part of him wanted to grab his cell phone off the table and walk out of the restaurant, but he did not.

"Amman?" Ayesha called and he looked up at her. "Are you fine?"

"Well…yes. What happened?" Amman asked, confused.

Ayesha shook her head and looked out through the glass window next to their table. *Snowfall!* she smiled. When they were finished with dinner, Amman asked, "Do you want something else?"

"It's snowing outside," Ayesha murmured.

"Do you want to stay here or go outside?"

"Let's take a walk. It'll be great for now," she said, staring out the window.

Both of them walked out of the restaurant with a smile on their faces. They could see people on the street with their hands up in the sky, feeling the first snow of the season.

"Have you ever seen snowfall before?" Ayesha asked while they walked by the road.

"This is the first time," Amman said. "But you must have experienced many, right?"

"Not many. But yes, I have."

Amman looked at Ayesha. As always, her hair were tied in a bun. He longed to see them unwound, left loose over her shoulders, but that was the last thing he wanted to say to her in that moment. Ayesha looked like…well, she looked exactly like she always did. Beautiful! The snowfall had only added to her charm and had made her look angelic.

"Because you've studied in London?" he asked quickly before she could say anything.

"I'm not even from Shimla," she said softly. For some reason, she had thought she'd not tell Amman about the kind of person he thought she was. She figured that this was a good time to come clean.

"What?" Amman's eyes narrowed. A shadow of confusion flashed crossed his face as he tried to put together the complicated puzzle that surrounded his perception of her.

Ayesha stopped walking. "My name is not even Ayesha."

Amman stopped two steps ahead of her. She paused, collecting her thoughts.

"It'll be terrible if you say now that you're a ghost. Especially since I'm involved," Amman said and laughed.

It was the month of November and the temperature lowered steeply with every passing minute. Ayesha didn't laugh at Amman's joke. He was soon to realize that he was speaking to none other than Ayesha, and she was hardly amused by such silly jokes. Amman took her hand in his and walked her to the stairs of a closed shop nearby. They sat under the porch light. Ayesha smiled a little and crossed her arms, astonished at herself for what she had revealed only seconds ago. Amman waited for her to speak further.

Chapter 7

"Amman?"

He turned to look at her.

"Have you ever been in love?"

Amman didn't respond.

"It's such a terrible thing, I tell you…a failure."

Ayesha stopped again. Her voice became more emotional as she went on.

"I always felt amazed by how people could fall in love, until I fell in love with someone myself. At least that's what I believed. To me, this seemed insanity when I saw people doing extreme things for their beloved. The feelings that love inspired in one always astonished me, that which made you go the extra mile… all for one person. It bewildered me, for some things were just beyond my comprehension. People swear off things and fight the world for their love. It all seemed a bit of a stultification while I was growing. I felt that love had something obscure about it which was difficult to infer, and it always intrigued me. Honestly, I also never felt the urgency to understand it thoroughly, for I was not allowed to fall in love with anyone. Therefore, I never nurtured the dream of having someone love me, or loving someone myself. I was not meant for it."

She took a deep breath.

"What do you mean *not allowed*?" Amman asked.

She straightened up a little and looked at him sadly. She went on.

"Noor–my mother gave me this name two days after my birth. She believed I had a certain connection with the Almighty when I was born and she named me this. I do not have any fond memories of my mother because she left my father when I was only five. I never asked my father why she left us, but Dania, my father's chauffeur's daughter, told me that my mother had eloped with her lover, abandoning my father and me. He had ferocious eyes, I still remember. You know, he would fume with anger at the mere mention of love those days. He had such a loud baritone voice, I always shivered in front of him, even though he barely scolded me or yelled at me…ever. For some reason, I could never gather the courage to stand up to him. He had such an intimidating presence over me for I was his only child."

Ayesha turned away, but Amman could see the sadness in her eyes. A part of Amman was sad now too, but he could not say anything at that moment.

"Outside the *haveli,* there was a small cottage where Dania's father Rasheed uncle lived. I haven't seen them for a few years now and Dania is getting married soon. Rasheed uncle has been around for as far back as I can remember. He told me that he had been around since my grandfather's time, who hired him as his chauffeur in the first place. My father was twenty years old at that time and his beard had just started to grow," she smiled. "Rasheed uncle was twenty seven. Despite the years between them, they were close…very close, in fact. Likewise, Dania was very close to me, my innocent confidante since early childhood. We grew up together in that same house, our *haveli*. After my mother went away, Dania's mother took care of me fondly, never differentiating between Dania and me. We were her two daughters. I remember how she used to feed me with her hands whenever I'd visit their cottage as a small child. She used to sing songs to us and called us her two little flowers. The memory which I hold most dear to me is when she used to make us sit on her lap and tell us fables of a princess and her prince. Of course, we loved it as children. I could not call her my mother for I was not born from her womb, but to me, she was my mother. Then one day, she left us too. She died."

Amman noticed her eyes swimming in tears, but she didn't weep. There was a brief silence between them.

"Do you miss her?" he asked.

Ayesha smiled as a tear rolled down her eyes. "Well, that's okay, I suppose," she said and turned her head to look at the people who had come out to enjoy the snow.

"I belong to a lineage of Nawabs. The Nawab of Awadh!" she started again. "My great-grandfather was a Nawab of Awadh sometime in the early twentieth century. Throughout my childhood, I never truly grasped the real meaning of a Nawab. I rarely had any meaningful father-daughter moments as a kid. I mostly just watched my father engaged in writing, painting and listening to Sufi music. The only thing of royalty that I truly experienced as a kid was hard discipline. This is also the reason perhaps that I could never understand my father deeply. He spoke very less, kept to himself most times, barely expressing his concern that he had a daughter too. He only spoke frankly with Rasheed uncle, that too when he occasionally drank in the lawns outside the *haveli,* but he just couldn't show his love or affection towards me. I felt more like a thing that needed to be protected, than someone to be loved. He was diligent and took it on as his duty to protect me from evil or worse. When I look back now, I think I always refrained from going near him a lot. We never shared any bond of love. I feel I was deprived of a loving childhood."

Amman nodded gravely. As she spoke, the only thing Amman could think about was 'not falling in love with Ayesha'. He looked at her and could tell that she was still finding words to say the rest.

"My father hardly ever kissed my forehead, except on my birthdays which he celebrated with great zeal among the aristocratic families of the neighbouring states and his family friends. A few of my relatives used to arrive from even New York and London. It always used to be a great ceremony for my father and his close associates. There used to be a lot of *sufi* music…I believe he was passionate about music, and Sufi music made up the little blithe nature of his psyche. I always wondered whether the celebration was indeed for me, or for his good fortune. I don't know whether it was my imprudence or my way of perceiving things around me, but I spent my childhood in a strange solitude."

"I reckon so," Amman said under his breath, not moving his eyes away from her.

"I never displayed any fury or sadness on my face, for I knew that it did not matter to him. I had to keep my displeasure for his conduct to myself. Whatever little I could share in terms of my secrets or my own melancholy, I did with the friend that I had found in Dania. And whatever love of a father or a mother I've received in my life, I gained it from Dania's mother. She cared for me and always remained humble for the entire time that I spent with her. I always feel that her death was as much a loss to me as it was for Dania and Rasheed uncle, for I had lost someone who showered unconditional love over me. Even though I was not the sole recipient of her love, she was the only one who conferred her love and affection on me in the most sacred way. I loved her."

"That must have been difficult," Amman muttered.

Ayesha smiled wryly. "It was devastating."

"But you don't have to punish yourself for what you received from your father. I'm sure it must have been equally painful for your father when your mother left."

Ayesha lit another cigarette and offered it to Amman, but he declined smiling.

"Life became monotonous for me as soon as my mother left us. The change in my father's behavior leaning towards seclusion was indeed the influence of my mother abandoning him, which

I found out about from Rasheed uncle much later when I grown up, but there was more to what had caused me a deplorable childhood. Whatever happened between my parents surely left a mark, but there were some questions which I struggled with my entire life after that. I had all the comforts of a perfect life, but I could not discern or decipher for myself these few unanswerable questions. They were baleful."

"And for that reason your father and you didn't get along…"

Ayesha chuckled. "There was a strange sort of strain between us. We never quarrelled, and as I have said before, I was a thing to be protected, more than someone to be loved."

"I'm sorry to hear that."

"Their separation left me destitute – for love. My father's loneliness and his seclusion also had an impact on my life while I was growing up."

Amman nodded, uncertain of what he could say.

"I always had this fear of how my father would react when he finds out one day that his daughter is in love with someone. What would happen then? I feared his rage and wrath against that person and myself. Would he beat me, scold me…he'd be full of scorn perhaps or might he even kill me? I always carried this fear in my mind as well as my heart. I still remember, Rasheed uncle used to drop me and pick me up from school everyday. He was always on time. He would come in our car, pick me up and take me straight back home. I used to watch other children indulge in fun and frolic outside the school, but I was not allowed to participate in it. I felt utterly deprived watching the other kids enjoying like that. And as things became more clear to me, that I could never have those moments of joy and mirth myself, my disposition towards them never went ahead either."

Amman could see that she was obviously not happy about it.

"Do you hold your mother responsible for all this?"

"It is what it is," she said simply. "A lot of it was the influence of my mother's elopement. I suppose, had she not escaped back then, the story of my life would have been different today. For a long time, I had this bitter and disoriented childhood. So yes, sometimes I do blame her for whatever I received at that time. To be loved by my mother and father was my birthright. But I only craved for it. The irony in all this was that all three of us lived a separate life. Every time I felt my mother's absence, it developed a feeling of contempt in my heart towards her. For a long time, I felt that I wanted to confront her. I needed my answers at that time, but I don't have any desire of questioning her anymore. I just wish to see her once before I die."

"So you didn't see much of her?"

"I hardly remember anything about her. She never came to see me herself." Ayesha smiled a little sadly. "And then I fell in love," she said.

"I'm sorry?"

Ayesha smiled. "At least that's what I thought."

"Thought?" Amman asked and looked at her again.

"Kind of," Ayesha said. "I completed my school education at eighteen and graduated at twenty-one. For higher education, I had my father's consent to shift to London and study International Relations from London School of Economics and Political Science. I remember, my father didn't want me to leave from his sight, whether out of love or a protective instinct, I don't know. But somehow, he gave in to my demand, albeit with a little reluctance, after some persuasion from Rasheed uncle. He played a small role in taking my petition on to fulfilment. That was my escape hatch. I wanted to break the monotony, to see something new, to learn something new. I felt desperate at times. I was not allowed to fall in love with anyone, for I was already betrothed to someone of my father's choice. To dream of someone in my life was never a solid possibility."

She cleared her throat, thinking of something for a moment, then continued, "I remember my father's bleak face the day I was leaving for London. He came into my room without even knocking on the door, the way he usually did. That day, he seemed very effusive in the words he said to me, and it struck me that very moment how his life was going to pass in absolute solitude from then on. What great fortitude he had shown his entire life, for I had never seen his fragile side. It pained me to see him teary-eyed that day.

"You will leave in the evening, right?" he asked.

I was staring out the window at Dania's cottage, for I was going to miss her. My father's intrusion into my room broke the silence and I turned around to look at him. He did not look at me directly in the eye, but I noticed the stolidity he carried on his face.

"At six, precisely," I replied. I had imbibed my father's brevity for words over all those years that I spent with him at the haveli. Looking at his sad countenance that day, however, I did not feel like going away from him, that too for such a long time.

"Rasheed uncle will go with you, alright?"

"You'll not come with me, Abbu?" I asked politely, and he gazed at me as if he was never going to see me again. I never could understand his psyche, or what he actually desired to convey through his eyes or his words. I always tried to get more words out of him, but he did not respond to my question. Instead, he looked at me gravely. It seemed unusual to me, for I expected him to give an answer in yes or no. So, I asked him again.

"Abbu, will you come with me to the airport to say goodbye?" I was curious by then.

"I'm sorry, my princess. I'd have surely come, but seeing you go away will be a little hurtful. I'd rather stay at home and wait for you to come back once you complete your education."

I had expected him to accompany me to the airport, however, his refusal to do so did not hurt me. I was hapless in love, and just nodded in agreement. I shook my head as my father left the room. Some part of me didn't want to leave him. I wondered at once if I was really going away from home for studies, or in pursuit of love? This thought alone kept me engaged for a long time. On my solicitation, my father had agreed to sending me away from him, and I had convinced myself that I could live my life on my own terms too. As the time of my departure inched closer, however, the thought that my father was going to be alone perplexed me more and more.

A little while later, I went to Dania's cottage. She was in the middle of offering her namaz. She was sitting on a mat, her head covered in a scarf and palms right in front of her face. Dania was a little chubby in her appearance. I looked at her plump fingers, her bright face and remembered her effervescent smile...I knew I was going to miss her and her gibberish talk. I always felt relaxed in her cottage, as if no one was watching me. It was always so calm there. I knew my sojourn in London was not going to give me that, so I took a moment and closed my eyes till Dania finished her prayers. It gave me that solace I needed and I smiled.

"Didi? "Dania asked upon finding me there.

"How are you?"

She came near me and gave me a tight hug. Like a sister.

"You're leaving today, huh?" she said. I noticed a little displeasure in her tone, but I didn't mind it.

"I'll be back soon, Dania. I'm not going to live there for my entire life. I'll miss our conversations though," I smiled, but I felt dejected inside.

Her gaze was fixed on me, while I looked around. She spoke really less that day, as opposed to her usual vivid manner. I wondered if it was my departure or something else that bothered her.

"What do you want to do after college?" Dania asked all of a sudden.

When she said this, I thought we were heading into a discussion about faith, love and maybe the uncertainty of the future, but I cut her off and asked instead, "Aren't you going to accompany me to the airport?"

"I don't know," she said, shrugging. "If Abbu allows me, then maybe..."

"Don't worry, he will. You are my sister after all."

I had always called her that all my life, and with her, I knew it came from the heart. Although, she always shrugged whenever I said it. I don't know if she ever believed me on it, but I believed her to be one.

"Noor, you absolute angel...come back soon, or Abbu will get me married to someone before you," she laughed. I managed a polite smile in response.

Her marriage was the one thing that I couldn't ever imagine because we had both grown up in the same haveli and I just could not think of there being a time when we would also drift apart.

She smiled, the changed the subject after a moment, sort of throwing me off track. "Do you think about the future, Noor?" she asked.

I was startled by her question because it sounded...so ordinary.

"What if you find someone there and fall in love?" she asked again.

I shrugged, a little wary of where she was heading with this. I had struggled with this thought for a long time before and when she confronted me with it, I wanted to dismiss it altogether. Every time this thought crossed my mind, I reminded myself of the bond I was tied to.

"I don't know. I haven't figured that part out yet."

I knew by Dania's glance that she was not convinced by my answer.

"You know, Dania, we're not allowed to breathe out of our boundaries. We breathe because we're allowed to. Love is not a thing we ought to think of. It's a mere illusion in our world and we cannot be the recipients of it."

"But that's wrong, you know..."

"You know what my mother did, Dania. After that, I don't see any point in glorifying love. Besides, Abbu won't approve of it and we both know it, don't we?"

I could tell that Dania didn't want to talk about it anymore from the way she kept quiet for the next few seconds.

Eventually, and very unexpectedly, she said, "Well, you'll get married someday, but not to a guy whom your father has chosen for you. Of course, not. You'll meet some guy and the two of you will hit it off, and he'll ask you to marry him, and you will say yes."

"Perhaps, we should leave it to time and let our fate decide what we are permitted to do," I said mildly.

"You will," she said.

"What?"

"...say yes. I know."

Her thoughts and beliefs seemed absolutely ridiculous at times, but she always said what she had in her heart.

"How do you know?"

"Because I pray for you. Always!"

When she said this, tears rolled down from my eyes.

"I will miss you, Dania..."

"You're absolutely silly."

"How about you? What do you want to do in future?"

Dania turned away and got that far-off gaze in her eyes that made me wonder what she was thinking, but it vanished almost as quickly as it had come. All the windows of the cottage were open and a cool breeze rushed in to ruffle through Dania's hair.

"I want to get married," she said quietly. "And when I do, I want you to be by my side and I want everyone there. I want my wedding party bustling with people."

"That's all?" Though I was not averse to the idea of marriage, but it seemed kind of silly to hope for that as your life's goal.

"Yes," she said. "That's all I want."

I wondered how simple and sorted someone's dream could be; no agony, no expectations from the future, and no derangement. It was one of the reasons why it was so easy for me to put up with her. She always seemed sorted and very specific with her dreams and life. It didn't matter how less she had in her life, she made the best of it.

"I'll miss you, Dania," I said finally.

"I'll write you letters, and I hope you come back soon." Dania took a pause, then said, "I'll be very lonely without you."

It was rare to see Dania on this side of the emotional spectrum. She was always this happy-go-lucky girl and I was certain to miss her miserably. I so wished to continue having her by my side.

We chatted for a while, then left for the airport. I insisted Rasheed uncle to take her along. We said our goodbyes there. I walked away from Dania in silence, though she hung around there for a few minutes and watched me disappear into the crowd.

The little time I spent in Dania's cottage that day made me realize that she was just like the rest of us. And the particularly good thing about her was that she always managed to hide her emotions in a way that I never could.

Chapter 8

Ayesha was sad for a long time and Amman kept looking at her. Seeing Ayesha sad made him feel like he was falling in love with her. The more he gazed at her, the weaker he felt. The snowfall had stopped by then and it had gotten quite late too. A few honeymoon couples were still out though, purchasing eatables from the roadside vendors. Amman didn't know what he could possibly say to Ayesha at that moment and he felt bad. He knew what kind of a person he was, but Ayesha…she was a mystery still, a hidden secret!

"What happened after that?" he asked.

"I realized what I wanted from life, but of course it wasn't something I was going to get easily," she chuckled.

"And why was that?"

"Like I said before, I fell in love."

"So you did find someone!"

"And lost. This guy approached me as if I was the last thing to be conquered in life. And yes, I fell in love with the wrong sort. It was foolhardy, wayward and passionate, and all of it doomed as soon as it had even started. I slipped away from my University hostel so many times and could be spotted on the streets anywhere."

"And you left him then?"

"As I said, I was a thing to conquer, and he had done that. He had won the battle and had left the kingdom to ruin. I wrote a great deal at that time, long scandalous poems, dripping with adolescent passion, some melodramatic and some terribly sad, you know, like abandoned lovers, that sort of thing. And I'm not proud of it. They all chronicle my disappointment with love. They speak of loneliness and sorrow in a way that one would never want to fall in love. There is a sense of struggle with my own childhood and the beating in love I took from someone."

"And you judge your own work?"

"That's what I've been told by people who've read them." She looked at a couple of kids whimsically roaming in the street. She didn't look at Amman for a few seconds. Her attention was drawn by the kids and she smiled.

"How old were you when all this happened?" Amman asked.

"Twenty."

Amman nodded.

"Are you going to form opinions about people and life based on these few incidents from your past?"

"Have I seen anything different in life that I could say I'm blessed beyond my wish?" Ayesha said in response.

Amman guessed Ayesha was used to it. To him, though, the sparsity of people on the street now made the whole thing depressing.

"Maybe it's the conclusion," Amman said and shrugged.

Ayesha turned to him and smiled.

"How's Dania now?" he asked suddenly. "And why did you choose the name Ayesha when you've been given such a beautiful name like Noor?"

"I thought it was the conclusion for you," she said.

"Well..." Amman shook his head. "Let's take a walk," he said and stood up, but Ayesha held his hand. Amman looked at her, his eyes narrowed.

"Wait..." she said. Her eyes looked as if they were beseeching for something. A look of confusion crossed Amman's face. "I feel relaxed here," she said, staring into his eyes.

Amman nodded without saying anything and sat back down.

"My home was in Lucknow. I spent my entire childhood there. It was when I returned after my studies that my father brought me here. I always used to come here during my summer holidays since we had property here. My father is an influential man, you see. Imagine, all the way from Lucknow to Shimla..."

"That must have come as quite a shock."

"It did surprise me at first, but there was hardly anything I could do when all the decisions of my life were being taken by my father."

"Still, you don't ask him why he brought you here?" Amman asked conversationally.

"I guess father didn't want me to stay there my entire life."

"But a life in Lucknow versus in Shimla is just the opposite. That must have been a major culture shock for you, no?" Amman was quite amazed at how quickly she had adjusted to this new life.

"It's been five years now. More than anything else, I was angry because Dania had to be left behind. She was my soul sister. The good thing, though, is that she's getting married next month. I'll get a chance to see her again," she smiled.

"That's great!" Amman said ecstatically.

"Will you come with me to visit them?" Ayesha asked suddenly.

Amman wondered whether that was even possible for him or not. He was supposed to leave for a new place the very next month.

"I'm sorry. I didn't even ask if you…"

"No…that's not what I'm thinking," Amman interrupted. "But the Lord seems to have a plan for me that I just don't know yet."

"I just assumed that it might be possible for you without even regarding your work schedule. So…" This was the first time, Amman noticed, that Ayesha was giving an explanation over such a small thing. He had come to believe that she was a reticent one–few words and no explanations!

"We'll see. I'm not sure just how my coming days will be, you know, after this journey," Amman said softly.

"But do you agree, for the sake of this conversation, that we shall remain on good terms, Amman?"

"It's needless to say," Amman responded, though he himself was in a dilemma over what those *good terms* meant. "What happened next?"

"I was twenty-four when father brought me here. The loneliness that I had been experiencing since my childhood grew deeper still and filtered into my writings, especially my poems. I wrote a great deal on loneliness earlier, my experience with the guy I met in London all culminating to one end. Depression! I took little interest in the people here, or in conversations, or in any sort of entertainment. Nina and Nihit somehow became friends, but that was it. I grew averse to meeting new people. There were times when I just stayed at home all day instead of exploring new places or meeting other people. Nina and Nihit both helped me overcome my depression. I resumed my daily routine gradually and have now simply accepted my life the way it is. I still feel incomplete, though, as if I have left an important part of myself back in Lucknow." She smiled sadly.

"And what about your marriage to the guy your father had chosen for you?"

"I refused to go head with that," Ayesha said.

"And your father agreed with your decision?"

"I don't know," she said. "But he never spoke about it again."

"Don't you think your father has been supportive of your decisions all your life?" Amman queried.

"I feel sorry for him at times. Well, mostly. Life has been hard on him as well," she said shrugging. "Yeah, somewhere…"

"Does it ever scare you?"

"What?"

"That you'll end up being alone in your life…"

"I don't know," she said, and was silent for few seconds. "Who knows? I just might."

"I pity the guy you met…"

"Why?"

"How could a guy leave a girl so beautiful as you for nothing!"

Ayesha laughed.

"Beauty has its own flaw perhaps. A pretty face does attract people and that's how you're judged."

Amman looked at her and thought that this couldn't be the only time when someone had said something like that.

"It wasn't just the pretty face I was talking about. It's your soul."

"Are you kidding me?" Ayesha smiled at him. "Who talks about the soul these days? It's rare to find such a thing in people."

Amman did not say anything and just shook his head.

"You don't agree with me on this?" Ayesha looked at him in a way as if she had said something inappropriate.

"Is your mother a disappointment to you?" Amman asked.

"I believe she's a punishment for something I've not done."

Amman sensed that she wasn't always modest. False modesty would anyway not suit her. Everything she had told him was her honest assessment of life. He felt she was unforgiving of her mother. Although he had not read her poetry yet, he assumed to be full of imagination, emotions, disappointment, the crests and troughs of young love, separation and broken promises. A little later, he said the same to her and added, "…and you're probably good at it too."

"If I had not written all of that, I'd have lost my mind. It was important to let out everything–my anger, loneliness and that feeling of disappointment which had stayed with me for too long," Ayesha said.

"Does your father know about all this?"

"Naturally, he doesn't. Though, he's aware of my inclination for writing. I believe he should not know all this."

"Why?" Amman asked.

"It will break his heart, and I'd be nothing more than a disappointment to him, especially after my entire childhood. He himself has stayed alone all his life. The difference between the two of us is that he kept himself in solitude willingly, while this part of my life was thrown at me."

Amman walked her back to the hotel with various things running in his mind.

"You're quite a listener," said Ayesha.

"Not really," Amman said. "I just didn't have a choice," he laughed.

"Thank you for listening to all my ramblings."

"Your life isn't a box full of secrets to me anymore."

"Yeah," Ayesha said as she shrugged and smiled on her own. "I guess so."

"So where are we heading tomorrow?" Amman asked.

"Let's see how adventurous you are!"

"I bet I can beat you."

"We'll see tomorrow."

Amman walked her to her hotel room and stood outside. Ayesha crossed her arms and smiled a little, looking as if she'd come in from an evening stroll, contemplating the beauty of the world.

"I had a good time tonight," she uttered slowly. "Thank you. I spoke way too much, more than anyone should be made to hear from me. Goodnight."

"Sleep well. Goodnight."

Amman realized that Ayesha could really drive a guy crazy sometimes.

*****

The next day, Ayesha took him for mountain biking from Rohtang La to Pass. They did paragliding below the Rohtang Pass as well, and every time she asked Amman if he was game for it, he said, "I'm game for anything you throw at me."

"I wish I could take you for rock climbing, shining and snowboarding, but the weather wouldn't allow us at this time," Ayesha said.

Amman's noble feelings that surrounded doing everything with Ayesha there did nudge him once, for he was falling for her. Even though he knew he was doing the *right thing*, his mind and heart said something else.

"I want to do every possible thing here. I wouldn't want to miss a chance like this," Amman said with mixed feelings of ecstasy and confusion.

"I know," Ayesha said and giggled. "I'll take you for trekking."

"Where?"

"Hampta Pass to Lahaul. It will take four to five days."

Amman smiled at her, returning to his old cheerful self. "That's okay."

The entire time he spent with Ayesha, the one thing which kept running in his mind was how could he possibly escape from her charm, from not falling in love with her? It became harder for him with each passing moment. Every time she asked for something, he could not say no to any of it.

In the following two weeks, Amman's life changed into a roller-coaster of sorts, primarily because of Ayesha, although he wasn't sure what she felt for him. All he knew was that Ayesha was fairly comfortable with him. They grew so much in each other's company and began feeling as if they had both known each other for years. Every time Amman joked around, Ayesha would elbow him in the ribs mischievously.

While trekking in Hampta Pass, Ayesha once asked him if he had ever had a girlfriend, or if he had ever been in love with someone before. Amman laughed.

"Why are you laughing?" Ayesha asked, confused.

"I have been expecting this from you for a long time. It just came a little late," Amman said.

"Were you expecting me to ask you this on our very first meeting?" she asked playfully. "We were nothing more than strangers back then."

"Well, I've never had a relationship sort of a thing, you know..."

"Don't tell me. A wanderer like you must have found many. You never even had a fling?" Ayesha asked and winked at him.

"Not really. I am usually never at a place for more than a month. I am constantly traveling."

"Oh…I see…" she said.

"I'd be lying if I say that I didn't like anyone. So many faces, so many beautiful faces, but I guess I just never had enough time. You've got to understand and know people deeply in order to love them. And those beautiful faces were only a passing fancy."

"I guess you probably were more into your traveling," Ayesha took a dig at him and laughed. "How could you not find anyone? I'm surprised!"

Amman wondered what she really meant by that.

"So, what's so important?" Amman asked to get over it as quickly as possible.

"Well, I don't know," Ayesha said, confused. "But you're such a nice guy that it's hard to believe what you are saying. Anyway, such is life!"

This made him wonder if that was how girls thought of him. He shook his head.

"Really? I didn't know that," Amman said.

"What?"

"Is that how anyone would think of me?"

"You don't believe you're a nice guy?"

Amman nodded, his lips pressed together. "I don't know. I just don't think about it."

Ayesha wasn't going to let him go that easily.

"You're a nice guy, Amman. You don't have to think about it."

It was then that Amman started to wonder even more whether Ayesha felt the same way about him as he felt for her. But he gave himself time and pretended as if she hadn't said anything about him. The stories kept getting wilder and funnier as Amman revealed more about his life and his journeys to the various parts of the country. He had started to feel quite close to her as he shared with her his experiences. Occasionally, he'd crack a joke or two to keep the conversation lively, and Ayesha didn't hold herself back either. She laughed out loud and grew solemn whenever he said something serious. Amman kept a check consciously that Ayesha didn't go back to her usual brooding and grave self. His company was the perfect therapy for Ayesha for she seemed to have forgotten her past and where she had come from. She was not the same girl anymore whom Amman had met a few days ago. She was boundless. She laughed uncontrollably at moments and lived as if she didn't give a damn about the world. Amman noticed it all.

"Do you ever just sit and listen to the sounds?" Ayesha asked when they were at the top of a mountain at Hampta Pass. She carried a cup of hot coffee in her hands. Amman sat beside her on a giant rock and looked above.

"What sounds?"

"Like the crickets chirping, or when the wind blows? Or do you ever just lie on your back and stare at the stars?"

Amman smiled and said, "No."

"What are your memories made of, Amman, from all the places you've been to?" she asked as she took a sip of her coffee.

"Not the sky or stars, definitely. I mean, I've been to these places because I've loved traveling all my life and this was the only thing I wanted to do. I live like a friggin nomad, relocating every other month to a new place, and the rest is all detail to me. I remember the people I meet along this journey, and those who were around when I was growing up. When I say along this journey, I mean the ones I have lost on the way, as well as the important ones whom I have kept close, while also making new friends. If you ask me what my memories are made of…they're made of people. And they live in me."

Ayesha looked at Amman and smiled. She had been surprised by Amman's answer.

"I thought your memories would be made of the places you've been to."

Amman laughed.

"So the travel writing that you do, do you also write about these people?"

"Not precisely. But yes, I do have to write about how people are in the particular regions or places…"

"Not characters?"

"Not characters," Amman said. "I mean, I'm not writing stories to be heard or read."

She nodded.

"Although, I'd like to read your poetry someday..."

"They're a disaster, I tell you. They're not worth reading. Besides, a man who's full of life like you will find no pleasure in it. That I'm quite sure of."

"I see," Amman said and gave a slight nod.

"There's a part of me in those poems which I wouldn't want anyone to see."

"Does it scare you?"

"I believe I'd be judged based on those poems. They're too personal for anyone to read."

"Are those poems so bad?" Amman asked.

"I'll say, rather theatrical."

They shared a brief grin.

"I think you should stop being so judgmental about your own work."

"You always joke."

"I'm serious…" Amman laughed and tried convincing her further, but Ayesha didn't pay any attention to it.

"Don't worry, I'll write something fancy or glamorous very soon and then I'll give it to you."

Amman looked at her with a twinkle in his eye. "You mean, I'd fit right in there…in that fancy world of yours."

"I didn't mean it that way," she said quickly. "But yes, it will be pleasing to you," she winked.

"I doubt if I'll ever get to read them."

"You never know, Amman," she said, smiling. "What the Lord's plan is."

She looked into the distance as she said this, then glanced up at Amman for a moment before finally getting up and starting to walk towards their hotel.

As Amman watched her go, he couldn't help but think that of all the times he'd chatted with her, this was the friendliest conversation they had ever had. Despite the oddness of some questions and answers, Ayesha seemed practically normal, not haunted by her past and optimistic.

*****

After five days of trekking, they moved towards Spiti, another chunk of Tibet marooned in India.

"I spoke to Nina this morning," Ayesha said while driving. "Nihit is alright now."

"That's great."

"And I spoke to father as well…"

It was the first time that Ayesha had made a call to her father on her own.

"Did you?" Amman was visibly excited at the mention of Ayesha speaking to her father.

"He's fine, I think," she said. "But he said something which I've never heard him say for anyone before."

Amman looked amused and puzzled. "What did he say?"

"He misses me," she said sincerely. "Even though my father's a stranger to me, at least he feels this."

"Do you miss him? Ever?"

"Sometimes. Specially since I grew up without him around." Ayesha looked at him as she said this, then faced forward again. She tied up her hair in a bun a moment after. Amman noticed that she did this whenever she felt confused or wasn't sure what to say.

"Don't get me wrong, Amman – I love my father. It's just that at times I wonder what it would have been like to have my mother around. I think she and I would've talked about things which I never could with my father. You do know that a mother is always a girl's best friend, don't you?"

Amman didn't know what Ayesha was talking about, but he was happy to see that she had opened herself up to him in a way he had never imagined. There were more conversations between them than silence now.

"I think you'll like my father once you get to know him," she said. "I'm not saying that you have to meet him, but if it ever happens, I'm sure you'll like him."

"How would I get to know him?" Amman asked.

Ayesha didn't answer, but just smiled to herself, as if there was some secret that she was keeping from him. Amman hated it though.

After hours of journey, they reached their destination where villages were few and far between along the serrated moonscape where they arrived like mirages. Clusters of whitewashed homes sat huddled by green barley fields below monasteries perched on crags a thousand feet above. They could see a steady stream of motorcyclists and mountain bikers pit their machines against the most challenging road in India. They stayed at a homestay for the night and got a taste of the Spitian life, sleeping in a traditional whitewashed house and eating home-cooked food from the family kitchen.

"This wasn't exactly a part of my plan," Amman said while they stayed in Spiti valley.

"You have a chance of experiencing the unplanned. Most people know about the commonly visited places already. I'm trying to show you something beyond that," Ayesha said as she lay on her bed.

"I'm sure you've seen this place..."

"No, but it offers me a chance to be a part of things which I would never have seen if not with you," she said cheerfully. "Look outside; it's a beautiful night for strolling, isn't it?"

Amman looked around and said, "Yes, it is."

"Let's take a walk. Come!"

"Wait, aren't you tired?" he asked innocently.

"Just come!"

Amman put on a jacket and climbed down the stairs. Ayesha was waiting for him outside. She saw Amman's tall frame making its way towards her.

"Goddamn, it's cold here!" Amman exclaimed. He stuffed his hands in his pockets, wondering why Ayesha had called her out at this hour.

"You're in a good mood," Amman said.

Ayesha flashed her perfect smile at him.

"Ayesha, what if your father comes to know that you're with a guy alone far away from home? Don't you fear that? I mean, given the kind of life you've lived…"

"Sure, I do. But I'm not going to say this to him. Will you?" Ayesha turned to him and smiled.

Amman wondered if this was the perfect moment for him to confess his love to her. He could practically hear his heartbeat in his head. Laughing inside, he looked around. He thought, there was no way he could let this opportunity pass.

"Amman?"

"Yeah…"

"Are you feeling good?" Ayesha asked.

"I'm good. Yes. How are you feeling?" Amman felt his heart suddenly beating faster and his fingers trembled. He couldn't understand why it was happening to him all of a sudden.

"You know, I was thinking if we'll ever meet again in life after this journey…"

"What?"

"Yep," Ayesha said shortly. "You'll be traveling again to some other place after this, and then you'll meet some new people."

"Why are you saying all this?"

Ayesha shrugged. She was always very calculative before saying something, though in the past few days she hadn't been so with him.

"I think I'll miss you!"

They both became quiet. Amman took a minute and said, "We'll meet. I'll come and see you again in these very mountains," Amman promised.

"I doubt it," she snapped.

"Look," Amman didn't let her finish and turned to face her. "I've spent a long time with you here. And this is the first time I've ever been with someone on a journey for this long. To tell you the truth, it feels good to be with you here." Amman went on talking further as it had been building up inside him for a long time. "And the only reason I'm saying all this is because I really…"

"Really?" Ayesha looked at Amman.

Amman smiled and shrugged.

Ayesha took a step towards him, pulled him in a hug, tightened her arms around him and finally kissed him on his lips. It was a moment he could only have dreamt of and had probably waited for with baited breath. A few seconds later, Amman finally looked at her.

"You took a promise from me that I should not fall in love with you…"

Ayesha ignored what he said and looked up at him. "You won't say it, but I know you love me."

Here we go, Amman thought to himself.

"I think all this was in the Lord's plan somehow. What do you think of it?"

"I think of nothing at this moment," Amman said and pulled her close to himself. There was a moment of tenderness between them as they both kissed under the moonlight. Neither said anything and Amman's eyes were on Ayesha's face. She wasn't the shy sort of girl, but there she was…almost timid in his presence. In one frenzied motion, he grabbed Ayesha around her waist and lifted her up, still not removing his gaze from her face.

"Do you love me, Amman?" she asked, despite knowing that he did.

" I have since the very first moment I saw you," Amman said finally.

Ayesha had forgotten how the whole thing started. They looked at each other for a long time as if for the first time.

"You're beautiful," Amman said to her. "You look like an angel!"

That night was cool, the wind crispy and the sky absolutely clear without a hint of clouds. Back at their room around midnight, Amman's jaw dropped a little and he kept looking at her while she lay in silence next to him on the bed. He just kept looking at her for what seemed like a long time, shocked into silence by what had happened just hours ago. He wondered if Ayesha had felt the same for him as he had felt for her all this time. He held her hand and she smiled, as if they were holding secrets close to their hearts. He suddenly remembered that he had very little time left with her and that he would have to move to a new place very soon. He took a deep breath, then slowly let it out.

"You'll not sleep tonight?" Ayesha whispered with a gentle smile on her face.

Amman knew she was happy, in a way that he could never have imagined her with him. He shook his head and said, "No."

"I didn't want to regret it, you know," she said slowly, her eyes closed.

"I know."

She looked at him, as if wondering whether to believe him or not.

"Did you mean the things you said?" Amman asked.

Ayesha had her eyes fixed on him.

"When you said that you knew I love you?"

She began to smile.

"Tell me?"

"I could see it in your eyes all this while."

"You did?" Amman looked at her curiously.

"So?" Ayesha said with a mischievous grin on her face.

"I guess you know me more than I do myself," he said simply. He was stroking her hair as he whispered, "You have always been in my head since the day I first saw you." A minute later, Amman said, "Do you remember the things you said when we left Shimla?"

She nodded.

"And now you're here in my arms. What made you think that I'll not fall for you? I couldn't think of anything besides you…"

Ayesha saw the look on his face. "It is God's plan, like I said. I hadn't planned on it," she said stoically.

"I'm not going away from you now," Amman said. Though it was something he had never imagined he'd say to anyone, the words came out naturally as he gazed at her. Because of Ayesha's presence, it became something really special.

"How I wish that were possible, but I'll not stop you. What you do is something you love. I won't ever stop you from doing something you've always loved. I'm not going anywhere either. I'll wait for you to come back someday…for me." Ayesha's eyes supported the truth in her words. One look was all it took, and Amman couldn't help but feel sorry for himself. For a moment, he was confused. He didn't know what else he could say except promise that he'd come back for Dania's wedding in a few weeks. "…and that I promise to you," he said.

"Will you?" she asked, her face brightened.

He nodded. "I'm not sure how your father would react if he came to know about me…" Amman said. But Ayesha was joyous as she looked at him.

"Don't worry, it's going to be fine," she said and planted a kiss on his cheek.

"Do you think that's enough?" Amman asked innocently.

"What?"

"Attending Dania's wedding?"

"I'll be glad if you do," she said and smiled.

Amman knew for once that it was the right thing to do.

Chapter 9

It was the beginning of December and winter was at its peak, but the one thing that glowed warm amidst this cold was Amman and Ayesha's togetherness. The one thing that Amman liked best about Himachal was the fact that winter and snowfall seemed to last practically forever. The weather was a bonus for them, as it gave Amman a chance to explore all the places at the most beautiful time of the year. A few weeks passed, and Amman and Ayesha got into the easy habit of being together when they needed each other, and apart when Amman needed to be on his work. He had travelled through the entire valley within a span of a few days with Ayesha, and had now moved to Malana, the traditional mountain village. He spent a few days with the villagers there and watched them perform their traditional rituals. To get the most out of the cultural experience and avoid breaking any rules, he travelled around the place with a knowledgeable guide named Lama Dugh most of the time. The guide told them about a place with the same name as his somewhere near Manali. They spent three days in guest houses above the village, then headed towards Kasol, staying overnight at a home-stay in Rashol en route.

The next morning, they reached Kasol.

Spread out along the lovely Parvati river and with a mesmerising view of the mountains to the northeast, Kasol was the main traveler-hangout in the valley. It was a small village, much to Ayesha's liking, overrun with reggae bars, bakeries, internet cafes and cheap guesthouses catering to a large hippie Israeli crowd. Amman was quite astounded when he reached there. It wasn't what he had expected in a place like Himachal.

"Now, I wasn't expecting this," Amman said as he took in the diverse nature of people who thronged the city. "I had always heard of this place, but the real experience of it is something else entirely."

Ayesha looked at him. "It's okay. How could you've known?"

"Well, look who we have here…" A voice followed them and a jeep stopped next to where they stood. A man leaned over the steering wheel so he could see Ayesha's face. He had his hair tied in a bun and a long beard covering his jaw. He wore a colorful vest that partially covered his richly tanned skin. Amman noticed that the guy wore a lot of bands and bracelets on both his wrists and had ornamental chains rolled around his neck.

"Hello Taji," Ayesha said cheerfully.

"What are you doing here, girl? It's been so long…"

Ayesha looked around and smiled. "Yes, it is…"

"Is he your friend?" Taji asked.

"Yeah, he's a travel writer and we're exploring this place," Ayesha said.

"Man, it's really nice out there. I hope you like this place…"

"Well actually, we've just arrived here. So, this is all very new to me," said Amman.

Taji sighed and glanced towards Ayesha as she shrugged. "I'd offer you a ride, but it wouldn't be half as nice as actually walking under the stars, and I wouldn't want you two to miss it."

"Don't worry, Taji. I'll show him around…"

"Hey girl, we're all going to my place anyway," Taji said. "Would you like to meet us there? You know we've got plenty of stuff there..."

"Oh, no…that's alright. We were just heading to our guest house."

"Cool. You know where to come if you need something, right?"

"Oh, don't worry. We won't need it," she said innocently.

"Alright! I'll leave the two of you to it then. I should probably get going," Taji said. "Hey, enjoy your stay here!"

Taji turned the key in the ignition and got the car rolling again.

"Thanks for stopping to say hello," Ayesha said and waved.

"You already know people out here, huh?" Amman said as soon as Taji left.

"Yeah, some old acquaintances. I used to come here very frequently until last year."

"You could've gone to his place. I'm sure you would have found some old friends there," Amman said casually.

"You do know what sort of place that is, right?" Ayesha asked.

"I have a fair idea," Amman said sarcastically and looked at her.

"I doubt it," Ayesha snapped.

"Did he mean marijuana?"

"Every possible thing that you can imagine…"

"You don't miss a thing, do you?"

"Now I don't," Ayesha said. Amman sensed a hint of sadness in her voice. "There was a time when I came to this place like every six months. Nothing seemed right in life then, you know, and I took on this hippie lifestyle, maybe to forget the past. It just gave me an escape, a means to forget everything that had once bothered me. And then, I just accepted everything as if it was nothing. Do you know what I mean?"

"I'm glad it worked out better for you…" Amman said.

Ayesha smiled and reached for Amman's hand to lead the way. "Come with me," she said.

Amman explored the entire area within two days, dividing his time fairly between old and new Kasol, and that felt enough to him for his assignment. At once, he wondered how the days had passed with Ayesha by his side, and imagined how it'd all have gone had he been alone for days in those mountains and terrains that he saw in Spiti valley. He had always traveled alone his entire life, but the sudden arrival of someone had brought so many changes with it, that it only left him asking for more. However, he often found himself pondering over what he would do next, after all this? Somewhere, he feared that he would lose Ayesha. It was the first time that he had started to think of losing someone, and the thought ached his heart. At times, when he went out alone for a walk, he missed her presence next to him. He contemplated over telling Ayesha what was going on in his mind, but wondered how she'd react, whether she'd laugh it off, or whether the speed of his thoughts would scare her. The more time he spent with her, the more he thought about talking with her about this. But despite everything, Ayesha had been nothing but kind to him, and he could not bring himself to hurt her.

Their last day in Kasol was also the day of Christmas and Ayesha's friend Taji insisted that they spend the evening at his place to celebrate. He had come to visit them at the guest house they were staying in.

Later, when Amman asked her if she was comfortable going there, she refused.

"Let's go. He has invited you twice now. We'll only stay there for an hour, then come back, okay?" More than Ayesha, it was Amman who seemed excited to go there, and Ayesha just didn't have the heart to turn him down.

Since they had not carried clothes appropriate for a party, Amman put on his hounds-tooth jacket to go out and shop while Ayesha waited at the guesthouse. He bought a nice short pink dress for her that he found after a tedious run-around at the city's market, realizing soon enough that buying clothes for a girl wasn't exactly the easiest thing to do.

They were supposed to be at Taji's house at seven, but because of this matter with the clothes, they arrived a few minutes late. The door to his place was locked and it didn't seem like a Christmas party from outside. There was no music and the place seemed completely desolate. They had to pound on the door a few times before Taji finally heard them and opened the door a moment later.

"Ah…you're here," Taji said happily. "We've been waiting for you. C'mon, everyone is here."

He led them down the hall to the rec room, a place where Ayesha had been before in some of her previous visits.

"You do remember this place, girl, don't you?" Taji asked as he kept walking.

"Quite. It's still very much the same," Ayesha said.

Amman paused for a moment to exhale deeply before finally heading in.

It was better than what he had imagined though. In the center of the room, there was a giant tree decorated with tinsel, colored lights and a hundred different handmade ornaments. It wasn't the sort of Christmas tree one usually expected to see, but it was good. Beneath the tree were wrapped gifts of different sizes and shapes spread in all directions. They could see the stash of weed and marijuana they had as well. There were people all around the tree, some of whom were sitting on the floor in a small semi-circle. Not all of them were dressed as sophisticatedly as they both were. In fact, Amman was amused to see that he and Ayesha were the best dressed there. Everyone else was casually dressed in jeans and t-shirt. A handful of them were wearing shirts, while some girls were in shorts and skirts, but Ayesha looked particularly angelic.

The music was loud, most of it just trance. On the table beside the door, there was a bowl of cookies and pastries shaped like Christmas trees and sprinkled with sugar. Amman could see a couple in that bedlam kissing, the girl sitting on the boy's lap.

People were enjoying and having drinks as they listened to 'The Night Before Christmas'.

"Hey buddy, just make yourself comfortable in here..." Taji said as he handed a glass of beer to Amman, patted his shoulder and disappeared amidst people the next moment. His eyes searched for Ayesha for a few seconds till he finally located her. She was sitting on the floor in front of the tree, her legs folded beneath her. To Amman's surprise, she had her hair untied which hung loose over her shoulders. He hadn't noticed this at the guest house.

"You found a book here? I'm surprised," Amman said as he reached her.

"Just caught my sight. I'm surprised too, by the way," Ayesha said.

"I'm sorry, I started without you," Amman said. "I'm glad you agreed to come here with me," he said, admiring how wonderful she looked.

"I don't know most people here. Taji is the only guy I know from before."

"Well, I guess we both are aliens here then."

Ayesha held his hand and said, "I don't need to know anyone as long as I have you by my side."

Amman sat down on the floor next to her, kept his glass of beer aside, and took her hand in his.

"Isn't this a miracle?" he said and looked into her eyes.

"Who knows..."

"Maybe it was somehow in the Lord's plan, as you've always said," he said. In the warm glow of Christmas lights that shone on her face, she looked more pretty than anyone he had ever seen before.

She smiled at him softly.

"But tell me, Ayesha...why me?"

"I don't know. It just felt good to be around you from day one.

It's true though that bringing you here on this trip wasn't the plan…but it just happened. We could've gone back with Nina and Nihit at the start itself, but something stopped me. I just couldn't do it," she said. "If you ask me the reason, I wouldn't be able to give you one."

They sat quietly for a moment and Amman returned his gaze to the lights once again.

"Can you make me a promise, Amman?" Ayesha asked, keeping her voice low.

"What?"

"Never promise me anything in life. I don't want you to make any promises to me," she said earnestly.

His eyes narrowed and he wondered what that meant. He glanced at her, not knowing what to say.

"Thank you for not asking what it means."

"Though I want to know, of course," he said.

"No. It's just one of the things which I don't want you to do."

Amman already knew what was inside her and that she feared for something, but he couldn't believe that she had said it already.

"Do you fear that I'll leave you?" Amman asked breathlessly. "Because I'll move to a different place in a few days, that's why?" Compared to the joy he had seen in Ayesha earlier, he didn't expect to hear this so soon.

"Because people make promises and they destroy the sanctity of love. I don't want you to do any such thing."

"That's all? I knew it…" Amman said, but Ayesha interrupted.

"No, Amman. No. I know you'll be traveling to new places and then it won't be the same."

She looked towards the Christmas tree and Amman's eyes followed her gaze. "This relation will be without any promises. We'll let our destiny choose its course."

"But I don't believe in fate and destiny, Ayesha. Now is the only moment that I have with you. You're with me in this moment and for all the moments yet to come in my life where we might not be together, I want you to know that you're all that I know of." Amman held her face and kissed her gently. She smiled at him and he smiled at her. All Amman could wonder was how he had fallen in love with a girl like Ayesha.

"Amman…" she asked, "Do you ever think about God?"

"Why?"

"I do believe that the Lord has a plan for us, but sometimes I just don't understand what the message could be. Do you think the same way as I do?"

Amman wasn't the kind of person who thought about life that way. He was the go-getter. If he needed something, he just made sure he got it.

"Well, I don't think that way. I believe we just have to have faith above all sometimes."

"I've been thinking about it a lot lately."

"I think you've been thinking about a lot of things lately. You shouldn't do that."

She nodded and smiled to herself.

"What? Have you guys been sitting here and talking to each other the whole time? Come and enjoy with us!" Taji came and broke the silence. He dragged them up by their hands and said, "Let's dance, c'mon!"

Amman took a sip of his beer in an attempt to soothe the sudden dryness in his throat. Meanwhile, Taji changed the music and played Bryan Adams' *Let's Make A Night To Remember.*

The room was filled with people and music, and Amman knew this was the last night he was going to be with her. Without saying anything or uttering another word, he pulled Ayesha closer to him and danced. He recalled the evening when he had first seen her, drenched in rain, her hair untied and a mystic beauty about her. He thought of the night spent in Manali when Ayesha had poured out her heart to him and remembered how angelic she had looked that night. As those images were going through his head, his breathing suddenly went still. He looked at her in a way that he was going to miss her. He remembered how he had once said that he didn't know what missing meant. Now he knew. It was the last night of their journey, and both were a bundle of emotions. He didn't know what to make of it. Ayesha looked at him with a peaceful countenance, smiling but far away at the same time. Amman's arm was tight around her; her breathing was shallow and weak. The sky outside the window had grown dark, but twinkling lights were now starting to appear in the distant sky.

"I know what you're thinking, Amman," Ayesha said. She gently kissed both his cheeks and then finally, his lips. "That," she said, "…is exactly how I feel about you."

Chapter 10

A month had passed and the journey came to an end. Ayesha had made it really special for Amman in a way that he had never thought. He had a smile on his face, a joy which he had never felt before she came into his life. While Amman was happy, cherishing the time she had spent with her, Ayesha's eyes were a little moist, as they had been that night in Manali.

Upon reaching Shimla, Ayesha stopped the car in front of Amman's old hotel. She burrowed herself in his arms and they held each other for a long time as if they were never going to let go of each other. The people around looked at them, but they didn't care. Amman observed that the *right thing* wasn't so bad after all.

"Thanks for inviting me on this trip," Amman said.

"Thanks for being you," she turned to him and said.

"What are you going to do now?" Amman sighed and asked.

"I don't know. Maybe…I'll write new poems," she said.

"Make sure you don't go back to writing what you described to me the other night. Not like the said ones," Amman said and held her hand, not hard but enough to let her know what he meant. "I love you."

"I hope you come for Dania's wedding," she said softly.

"As long as you want me to come, I'll be there."

She squeezed his hand back, looking radiant as ever in the evening light. "I love you, Amman," Ayesha said. But this time, she seemed frightened.

"Know that we'll see each other very soon. You don't need to worry about anything," Amman said and kissed her hand.

"I'll see you soon then," Ayesha said with a gleam in her eyes, though they were moist still.

"Yes. I'll see you soon then."

After they finally let go of each other, Amman proudly motioned his hand in a gesture of love and saw Ayesha growing back into her cheerful self. Even after she was gone, her pretty face kept returning to his mind.

A couple of days later, Amman met Zafar at his restaurant. They greeted each other and made their way into the restaurant. Zafar flickered his eyebrow at one of the guys working there. "Bring some tea, Aslan."

"Oh, it's not necessary," Amman said, but the boy had already disappeared into the kitchen. Amman looked around, toying with his hotel room's keys.

"It's great to see you again," Zafar said cheerfully. "I didn't expect to see you, you know. I thought you might have left this place. It's been two months now."

"I didn't," Amman said. "It's been a journey to remember, if I tell you. Not the kind I expected at all."

Zafar nodded. "I hope it was good…" he said.

"It was close to perfect, to be precise. And if I tell you whom I completed it with, you'll be surprised."

"That's news, huh. Tell me then."

"Do you remember the girl I saw in your café the very first day I came here…"

Zafar watched Amman with a smile across his face.

"Her name is Ayesha. Well, actually Noor."

Amman told the entire story to Zafar over the next hour, even the minute details of the journey and about Ayesha that he could remember. He told the story as if the bond between them was no ordinary affair of love, but the most precious thing in the world. Zafar's patience with Amman and his story was boundless. In the end, he gazed at Amman with confusion.

"So, what are you planning now?" Zafar asked.

"I don't know. Do you think it's all going too fast?" Amman asked.

"I hope you haven't made any promise to her yet…"

"Why would you say that? And promise of what?"

"Marriage. Don't you know, Amman…women are emotionally and practically immature."

Amman considered what to say for a moment, opting to remain quiet at first, then said, "She isn't like that. And I know because she herself asked me not to make any promise to her."

"What?"

"Probably, she fears that I'll leave her like all the other people in her life," Amman said gently.

"And what do you have to say to that?" Zafar asked smiling.

"Man, you're asking too much now…" Amman said and they both laughed.

"But that's the inevitable, Amman. You'll have to think of marriage if you love her. Don't you think so?"

"All I know for sure is that I don't want to lose her."

Zafar looked him in the eyes and said, "I think you should ask her for marriage."

There was a momentary silence between them.

"Look, I'm not saying that you've to marry this girl right now. But eventually, you'll think about it. And then, think from the perspective of a father. I'm sure he won't wait for too long either. You should marry her," he said. "Well, before you lose your looks."

Amman smiled at this. He told him that his mother used to say the same thing to him.

"Now she doesn't?"

"She gave up on me," Amman chuckled.

"Well," Zafar said at last, aiming to ease the tension, "One of these days, you might just make a decision. Make sure it's not too late by then."

For a few minutes, neither of them spoke a word.

"Don't wait for too long. This is all I'm saying."

Amman looked at him. "No, I won't," he said, looking certain.

The rest of the conversation was mostly about what part of the state he was going to visit next and how Zafar's family was. He missed being around Ayesha, but he knew that it was for the best. Too much closeness wasn't good, he reminded himself.

On his way back to the hotel, Zafar accompanied him. Amman insisted on him to not bother himself with it, but Zafar did not care.

"Before you leave Shimla, I want you to come to my place for dinner. It'll be an honour."

"Sure!"

"Thank you," Zafar said.

"For what?"

"For not refusing the offer."

"Did you think I would?" Amman blinked.

"Well, who knows? You're like a bird, always flying to the unknown! And only God knows if we'd ever see each other in life again."

Amman smiled. He had always been told this by the people whom he met along the journeys he made. And he never had an answer to this.

"There's no destination for me, Zafar. At one moment, I'm here and the other, I'm not. There's a great price I pay for this dream that I'm living. If I put it in the right words, no matter how much I'd like to stay with all the people whom I meet on these journeys, I can't. I belong to all, yet to none."

"I can understand," Zafar said laconically.

"I've found a friend in you though," Amman said. "That I'm sure of."

"Yeah, you can cheer me up with these kind of words now," Zafar said and laughed.

"Shut up!" Amman laughed.

"Will you go there?" Zafar asked. "Lucknow?"

"Well, I'm trying. It's just a one-day affair for me, but I won't know anyone there."

"Make sure you do. It will be a good chance to get to know her more. A wedding always brings the true desire out of a girl. Don't miss it," Zafar said. Amman didn't quite get what he meant by *true desires*, but he knew what he had to do.

*****

Before Dania's wedding, Amman left for Dalhousie. He still had some time left for a small recce. He called Ayesha before he left Shimla to head to Dalhousie.

"What should I bring for Dania?" Amman asked. He was not aware of the customs and rituals of a Muslim wedding, so he asked.

"You don't need to bring anything," Ayesha answered from the other end. "Just be there, if possible, on the wedding day."

"Does your father know that a surprise guest will be coming to the wedding?" Amman asked jokingly.

"He doesn't know yet. Maybe it's for the best that I don't let him know," Ayesha said. "Or maybe I'll just tell him about you. I don't know how he'd react. He has not been keeping well for the last few days."

"What happened?"

"I think his age is catching up with him, although he's not too old."

"I see." Amman wondered if it'd be a good thing to tell him about their relationship at this time. "You know, if he's not keeping well then don't tell him right now."

"I'll see." Ayesha kept quiet for a moment. "Don't worry. I'll figure something out," she finally said, trying not to show her disappointment over it.

"Of course, you will."

"I told Dania about you, though."

"You did?"

"And she's waiting to meet you now."

"Well, did she say anything to you?"

"She was so happy the moment I told her that I've met someone recently. I think she forgot for a moment that it was her wedding and not mine."

Amman let out a short laugh. "Tell her that I'm equally excited to meet Ayesha's sister."

"And there's one thing I forgot to tell you…I'm still Noor for her. She calls me by that name."

"I see. That means, she doesn't know that you're Ayesha here?"

"She does. And she asked me bluntly if I've found a lover…"

"What did you say?"

"That there's not a thing wrong with her."

Amman grinned on the other side of the phone.

"You should go now. We'll leave from here in about a week. I hope to see you there!"

"You will," Amman said. When they finished, Ayesha thanked him again and told him that she would get in touch with him again soon.

*****

Amman was left with only a few days in Himachal, after which he had to be in Lucknow for Dania's wedding. Beyond that, he himself had no idea where he was going to be. Deep down, he knew that the coming days were crucial for Ayesha and himself. He often thought back upon the time he had spent with Ayesha, roaming in the mountains, just the two of them, and wondered how uncertain life could be. Ayesha had been a complete stranger to him when he saw her for the first time in Zafar's restaurant, then a few minutes later, they were acquaintances. How fate had played its part in turning them into lovers from strangers! He understood that Ayesha was a girl he couldn't go wrong with, and although there was no promise between them, he knew too well that the *no promise* thing somehow attached him to her and it was absolutely fine. He knew why Ayesha had maintained this equation between them, and it kept coming back to him. The tough task ahead now was meeting Ayesha's father and getting his consent for their relationship. He didn't fear for himself, but for Ayesha, so she wouldn't get hurt if it didn't go as per her wish.

There was a heavy snowfall in Dalhousie during his stay there, and even a regular uneventful life there seemed beautiful. It was also the time when phone lines didn't work properly, which was sometimes exasperating, but then he always pictured Ayesha's face wanting the whole thing to go away.

With its plunging pine-clad valleys and distant mountain views, Dalhousie was another cool hilly retreat for him. And just like Manali, numerous modern style hotels there catered to honeymoon couples from the plains. After about two days or so, he realized that there wasn't a lot to do there other than strolling around, appreciating the crisp air and the hilly view. He saw a few Tibetan refugee houses in the town, and the painted rock carvings of Buddha along the southern side of the ridge.

Around Dalhousie, he visited the Kalatop wildlife sanctuary, Khajjiar and Chamba as part of his assignment, and was soon done with the work he had been assigned. He also reminded himself that it had been in fact really long since he last spoke to his mother who was in Mumbai. First, his traveling had made it difficult for him to speak to her, and then the bad weather deteriorated the conditions even further. He had been trying to speak to her for the last couple of days to tell her about Ayesha, but all was in vain. He wanted to visit her after attending Dania's wedding. He had received a text message from his mother one day, asking about his well-being and if he had forgotten to respond, but since then, all his attempts to contact her had gone in vain.

It was uncanny, the timing. On his very last day in Dalhousie, his phone rang with an unknown number. When he did not receive the call, it rang again. A local guide accompanying him asked him to take the call. "It could be important," he said.

"Yeah, maybe," Amman said and excused himself. "I'll only be a minute."

"Take your time," the local guide said.

Amman was inside a museum then and could see heavy snowfall beyond the window panes. He looked at a collection of miniature paintings from Chamba, Kangra and Basholi schools and cast a skeptical glance.

"Hello!"

A voice answered from the other end, "Is this Amman?"

"Who's calling?"

"Mr. Amman, I'm Dr. Abrol. I'm calling about your mother. She has had an accident."

It came as a shock to him, an absolute shock. He had never expected anybody to call him for his mother, and he could not understand it for a moment.

"What happened to her?"

"Well, we were wondering if you could come here as a soon as possible," said the doctor.

"Yeah, but what happened? Tell me..." A sudden look of perplexity washed across his face at the mention of the words *as soon as possible*.

"Oh, she fainted in her house. Her neighbors brought her here to the hospital."

"Is she fine? Can I talk to her for a minute...I mean, I've been trying to reach her for the last few days but...where's she?"

There was silence at the other end for two seconds or so.

"Doctor?"

"She's all right. She's on bed right now. We've given her some medicines so...I was saying if you could come here to see her..." The voice at the other end was breaking because of the bad weather conditions. The disturbance in the line made it hard for him to understand what the doctor was saying. Amman simply said, "Doctor, I'll be there. I'm in Himachal right now and the weather is terribly bad here, but I'm taking the next available flight. Just tell me she's fine..."

"She is."

"And how bad was it?"

"Accidents happen. The good thing is that she's fine at this moment."

"Will she be all right?" Concern grew in his voice.

"Yes. Make sure you reach here soon. She wanted to talk to you, but we gave her some medicines half an hour ago and she's resting now."

"I should be there tomorrow. I'm not sure if any flights would be available or not, but I'm coming, doctor."

"All right!"

After he hung up, Amman could feel his hands shaking. He sat on a bench nearby and held his face in his hands. He was puzzled because it was the first time that he had heard something like this for his mother. He could not fathom what this *accident* meant though. He felt bad, almost cursed himself with regret that he was not with his mother at this time.

"What happened?" asked the local guide as he saw Amman tense.

"It's my mother. She's not fine," Amman said. "How soon can I get the next flight to Bombay?"

"I don't know. I can't really assure you that you'll get a flight in this weather. It has been terrible for the last few days," the guide said.

"I don't have much choice at this moment. I must leave as early as possible. I'm going back to the hotel to pack my bags."

While on his way to the hotel, Amman thought of Ayesha. He knew it'd break her heart a little if he didn't attend Dania's wedding, but also hoped that she would understand the situation. The snowfall outside was growing more intense with every passing second. He feared if he'd even get a flight, as the weather had altered for the worse all of a sudden. The local guide accompanied him to the hotel and then to the airport. Gaggal was the nearest airport for him. He dropped him in a car, but Amman kept quiet all the way. He rummaged around his mind for a way to tell Ayesha about this.

"Are you fine?" the guide asked.

"I'm fine," Amman said, maintaining his composure. "I must thank you for coming with me to the airport."

"It's important for you, I understand," he said.

"I have to make an urgent call, but there's hardly any signal here."

"You'll be able to connect once we're out of Dalhousie. Phones generally don't get any network here during this season. It will be better once we reach Mcleodganj."

"I hope so," Amman said. "You could drop me at a place where the weather is fine. Don't put yourself in so much trouble for me."

"Why? It's absolutely okay. And don't worry, I'll drop you safely to the airport."

In the greyish glow of the snowy winter, Amman's teeth began to chatter with the cold. He noticed that the guide was absolutely fine though. He guessed he was acclimatised to the area, unlike him. He adjusted himself nervously in the car seat, but didn't utter a word.

"Amman, do you need a blanket?" the guide asked. Amman looked at him, and found him looking back at him. "You'll catch a cold. Get a blanket. It's in the back seat of the car," he added after a pause.

"Yeah, maybe," he said and took a deep breath.

"Is your mother alone in Mumbai?"

Amman wrapped himself in the blanket and said, "Yes."

"I hope she'll be fine soon."

Amman looked at him.

"I'm sorry, I don't know much about her, but she'll be fine. I hope you reach there in time."

Amman looked out of the window and knew it wasn't enough. He kept quiet during the entire journey. It was a grey day, cold and bitter.

After hours of driving down the road, Amman finally reached the Gaggal airport. He thanked the guide and gave him some money for having helping him in his dire hour of need.

It was very crowded at the airport, with people panicking over flights getting delayed or cancelled. It was New Year's time and many people had come out to the mountains for a vacation. Amman knew that it was a bad omen for him, and that which he feared the most to happen, turned into reality. All flights were cancelled for that day. A thick fog descended over the city when he reached the airport in the evening. He looked out the glass panels of the airport premises and stared at the runway. Lights were blazing and airplanes stood parked in their places.

Amman reminisced about the time he and Ayesha had talked about the things that happened in the month just past. He thought of the moment when he had held her hands, and the way she had kissed him that night in Spiti, the Christmas he had celebrated with so many friendly strangers and all the goodbyes. Many random things passed through his mind and it eventually drifted back to his mother's condition which he was only partially aware of. He wondered if anything in his life had ever been this perfect at once, knowing at the same time that the end could be entirely nerveless.

He made several attempts to reach Ayesha's phone, but did not succeed. There was the one time when he finally heard the bell ringing, but Ayesha did not receive the call. He left her a message that his mother was not well and he won't be able to make it to the wedding as he had planned. He apologised for the same too. He knew that Ayesha was not in Shimla anymore, but in Lucknow to participate in the wedding preparations, but that was all he could think of doing at that time. He called Zafar as well to inform him about the same and requested him to inform Ayesha about it if she visited his restaurant after returning from Lucknow. When he had first seen Ayesha, it all seemed like a beautiful dream and the days he had spent with her were nothing less, but this reality was the exact opposite and he feared every moment while he sat in the waiting lounge of the airport.

With that thought alone, he kept waiting for the weather to be okay, for his mother to return to good health and for a call from Ayesha. This certainly had not been his day as it came to an end. Of all the journeys he had been on, this particular day seemed to have been the longest. Perhaps, the one that tried him the worst.

Chapter 11

It was like seeing someone one had lost during childhood, but was found again. How people change in their appearance in just a few years! It hadn't been that long for Ayesha and Dania, but when they saw each other from a distance, it seemed to them like a dream which both had been weaving together since their childhood, but had abandoned mid-way. Their longing to see each other had been left arid like a parched barren land beseeching for rain. Dania was taller now and seemed a little more dainty the moment Ayesha's gaze fell upon her. She had curly hair and long defined eyebrows that met gracefully just above her nose. She was indulging in gardening outside the *haveli,* where only the caretakers lived now. Ayesha stopped short when she saw Dania, and her father approached her from behind. Ayesha grinned and her knees wobbled upon seeing Dania after five long years. She hadn't seen Ayesha yet.

Ayesha lingered for a moment and thought of surprising her, although Dania knew that Ayesha was coming.

"Go meet her. Why are you standing here?" came a voice from nowhere. It was Rasheed Ahmed Khan, Dania's father.

"Where were you, Rasheed uncle? You didn't come to receive us at the airport today…" Ayesha said and gave him a hug. "Salam-alay-kum, Rasheed uncle! It's so good to see you hale and hearty here. You've no idea how I've missed this place…"

As Ayesha looked closely at Rasheed, she noticed a few wrinkles around his eyes and the grey flecks in his hair, just like her own father.

"This haveli has been waiting for you. And just like us, every part of this land missed you…" he said. "I apologize for not coming to the airport. You know about the wedding preparations, don't you?"

"She does, Rasheed," said Javed, Ayesha's father, and laughed. "Go and meet, Dania. She'll be happy to see you."

Javed and Rasheed hugged each other like brothers. As Ayesha turned to see Dania, their gazes met and recognition rippled across Dania's face. Ayesha waived at Dania. *This is her. This is her.* She could feel her clamorous heart inside her rib cage, the twist in her stomach, and it was beautiful. They both walked towards each other and hugged. Dania kissed Ayesha on her cheeks. Her skin was soft. When they pulled back, Ayesha held her at a distance as if appraising a painting with pride. There was a film of moisture over their eyes. but they were alive with happiness. Dania had narrow shoulders and a delicate built, her face was as pleasant as ever, and her hair were pulled back taut in a headband. She was wearing jade earrings and a green scarf was wrapped around her neck. Finally, she grinned.

"It has been so long," Dania said.

"It's nothing," Ayesha said. "At last, to be with you! I'm so glad."

"I'm so glad too," Dania said. "How was your flight?"

"Come inside you two. You'll have all the time to do this," Javed said.

"I have so much to tell you, Dania," Ayesha said and smiled. "God, I missed you so much."

"It's so strange, you see!"

"I know. My entire life!"

Dania nodded with a smile.

"You look beautiful, Dania."

Later, as they settled inside the *haveli*, Dania walked into Ayesha's room. She kept looking at Ayesha as she found her sitting on a couch, reading a book. It was that moment which Dania had waited to witness for a long time–Ayesha's presence in the room…in the *haveli* again. She watched Ayesha with perfect clarity, holding a book in her hand and relaxing on the couch with her glasses perched over her nose, enhancing her beauty a little more.

"It's just…a little unbelievable," Dania started, "that you're actually here. I keep thinking that you'll disappear."

"Why?"

"I have been waiting for you patiently since you moved to London years ago. Over these years, I had this thing in my mind that I'll never see you again, especially when baba decided to take you away to Shimla. For me, that in itself was the end."

"I felt the same. It broke my heart when dad decided to take me there all of a sudden on my return from London. You won't believe it, but I almost felt that I wouldn't even get to see you in your wedding dress. But dad gave me this surprise two months ago when he broke the news of your wedding. I was so out of touch with everything here," Ayesha said as she put the book down and took off her glasses. "I was so happy and excited, that I didn't even sleep a wink last night."

Ayesha held Dania in her gaze and beamed at her, as if she was afraid that the spell would break if she looked away.

"You always stand so far away from me...come here now."

"I'm sorry," Dania said and laughed.

Ayesha asked her about the guy she was getting married to, and they talked about the many things that they had missed telling each other and caught up with their old memories. Dania told her that the guy had a small business in Mumbai, and that he handled the entire business on his own. She mentioned that she was happy with the union of the two families.

"He's a good guy. You'll like him when you meet him…"

Ayesha listened intently as Dania spoke about how the proposal had come and how the guy's family knew Javed Ali Khan.

"I see," Ayesha said at the end. She considered the situation for a moment, then asked, "You're happy, right?"

Dania spoke after a moment of silence, "Remember, we talked about it once that we'll let our fate decide what's written for us…"

Ayesha kept her gaze on Dania without uttering anything.

"Guess what, fate chose this for me and I am at peace… of course, happy too. Too many expectations also lead to heartbreak…sometimes. I've learned it through the gaps I've had in my life. Those periods of silence made me understand and appreciate the bare necessities of life – be it people or things."

Dania nodded. "I guess, I never gave it much thought."

"To what?"

"To what mother did…"

"Bah, of course you did. You spent all your life thinking about her and how your childhood turned out for you because of her."

"Yeah, but I was thinking of her in a different way. I've cursed her all my life, Dania, in ways that you cannot imagine."

"I know that."

"But maybe, she chose the best for herself. Although I'll never forgive her for what she did to me, she chose her life and love for herself. I see dad alone these days, his life riddled with gaps… everyday a mystifying story, a puzzle to struggle through. And I believe this is why he took me away from this place. He didn't want my memories of my mother to have an influence over me. But ultimately, this is what became of me. I did exactly what dad protected me from all my life."

"What do you mean?" Dania asked and looked at Ayesha's face, as if searching for answers.

"I fell in love…maybe with the right one!"

Dania looked at Ayesha's hands folded in her lap.

"I remember almost nothing about my mother, not her face, nor her voice. All I remember is dad being alone, feeling myself that I could never share things with someone, and that something was always missing from my life, something good! Something…I don't know what that was. That's all. Maybe it's time that I forget the bitter childhood I had…"

"Who's it?" Dania asked, quirking an eyebrow.

"I met him in Shimla just a few days ago."

Dania inched a little closer to Ayesha. "And have you planned on marrying him yet?"

"Oh, Dania! Not really. We haven't planned anything as such yet. It's only been a month since I have known him. But he's so full of life, you know. He's always traveling."

Dania smiled.

"Do you think dad will agree to this relationship if I talk to him about it?" Ayesha asked quietly. "I'm very nervous."

"It's understandable," Dania said. "But I think you should indeed talk to him. Who knows, we may just see a change of heart in him after all these years…"

"Maybe on your wedding day then?"

Dania happily nodded. "You should."

A day before the wedding, Ayesha tried calling Amman, but his number was not reachable. She tried calling him many times, even left messages on his mobile, but none got delivered. It got her worried at first, but then she thought that he might be on some work assignment at the moment, and would be with her at the wedding ceremony anyway, as he had promised.

The entire *haveli* was beautifully adorned with flowers varying from roses and lilacs to sunflowers and tulips. The entire place was filled with their essence. The front gates opened onto a wide asphalt driveway embellished with lights and flowers. From there, one entered into the high-ceiling'd foyer decorated with tall ceramic vases. The marble floor of the living room glistened wherever left uncovered by the red and black *Kashmiri* carpets. The *haveli* looked glorious and sparkled as if encrusted with diamonds the day before the wedding.

Dania's wedding dress was gifted to her by Ayesha's father, as he treated Dania like his own daughter. The very close relatives of Dania arrived that day and stayed at the *haveli* itself.

Much of the wedding preparation work had already been completed by then. All the guests feasted on various kinds of vegetarian and non-vegetarian dishes in the backyard. It was a beautiful lush green lawn, dotted with beds of flowers – jasmine, sweetbriar and tulips – and bordered by two rows of trees. On an ordinary day, one could just lie beneath those trees and listen to the breeze playing through the leaves above. During autumn, this place seemed more heavenly to Ayesha than any other place in the entire world.

The same night, Ayesha entered her father's room. He was sitting on his recliner, motionless and slumped backwards, his legs covered under a checkered wool shawl. He was wearing a black cardigan that he had buttoned all the way up over his shirt, which made him look both frail and old. Ayesha wondered what thoughts gave him company as he sat alone in his room for hours.

"Dad?"

"Ayesha…"

"What do you think about when you sit alone?"

He laughed. It was rare to catch him laughing, and Ayesha had hardly seen him happy about anything in his life.

"I was thinking about the wedding," he said. He pulled up a chair close to his recliner and said, "Come, sit."

Ayesha sat down erect, pale, and leaning forward from the edge of the chair, her knees pressed together and her hands clamped. Her eyes were glued to her father, as if she had only a few moments left with him.

"I think it's time that you get married too. Dania is leaving and…"

"Dania had gone from my life five years ago, dad. You took me away from her long ago."

Javed looked at Ayesha and his gaze lingered on her, as he had never had her interrupt him before.

"Didn't you, dad?" Ayesha asked.

Javed cleared his throat and looked away. He nodded slowly. "But you do understand why I took you away from this place," he said. "You'd always have missed something here had you stayed in this place your entire life."

"Regardless, you stole all that I had. Not that I don't know what happened, but you also took away what I had remaining with me. Dania was like my sister. You cared so much about what I did not have, but not what I did have!"

"I thought it was for your best. Although, I know you never liked it and I feel sorry for that."

Ayesha looked down and kept quiet. She didn't speak anything for a minute or two, nor did Javed.

"Have you thought of marriage yet?" Javed asked. "The guy we saw for you…"

"That's what I came to meet you for dad…" Ayesha interrupted him again. She was amazed at her own behavior, at how she was talking to her father. Before she realized it, she told her father all about Amman. The moment she said it, she wondered what it was that gave her the courage to say something that she had barred herself from since childhood.

"…and I want you to meet him once, dad. I love him," she confessed. "I mean, I know he loves me, and I want you to see him once."

Javed didn't say anything. He went quiet and into deep thought. This silence always made Ayesha frightened for the unknown storm that might come her way next, but she waited to let her father speak. Her heart started palpitating in a way it had never before.

"Does he mean that much to you already?" he asked.

"Yes," Ayesha said quietly.

"Well, what have you tried so far?"

"I don't understand…"

"Have you made any promises to each other yet?"

Ayesha thought about it for a moment, feeling a little confused. "It's nothing like that yet. We love each other and that's it."

Javed sighed and sat in silence, while Ayesha told him about how they had met in Shimla and that he had accompanied her with her friends, Nina and Nihit, on a road trip just a month ago. When she finished, a look of concern flashed across Javed's face.

"I worry about you," he said. "It's only been a month and…"

"I know, dad. But I'm not saying that I want to marry him tomorrow. I only want you to meet him once. For me. Please, dad. Is it too much to ask for…?"

"Okay!"

Ayesha looked up, surprised and unsure if that meant a yes or no.

"I'll meet him. When is he coming?"

Ayesha couldn't believe that the battle had been won. Lost in disbelief, she seemed to look right through him. It wasn't enough.

"I asked, when is he coming?"

"Tomorrow. I mean, he did say that he would join us for Dania's wedding…"

"I know you love this guy, Noor," Javed said finally, addressing her with her old name after so many years. And when he said it, his attention was focused on her again. "But I don't want to see you getting hurt."

Ayesha felt as if she had imagined that he had really agreed to meet Amman, and that too so easily. Her eyes began to water.

"I know you have seen me in a different light all your life, someone over-protective and even possessive maybe, unlike other fathers, but there was always a reason for everything. I wanted you to understand that with time."

Ayesha smiled with her eyes glossed over. She wanted to thank him, though she didn't. She could tell that her father wanted to be alone at that moment, but she hugged him tightly. She had never done this in her entire life, nor had her father. But that moment brought both of them closer to each other. She had always maintained her composure, not revealing her emotions that easily, but in the last month or so, a drastic change had come about in her demeanor. After all, Ayesha too had a heart that could melt at the slightest nudge of emotion.

When Ayesha glanced over her shoulder on her way out of the room, she was puzzled to see her father's face in his hands.

*****

"You must be joking," Dania said when Ayesha told her that her father had agreed to meet Amman.

"You really think I would joke about something like this?" Ayesha asked sincerely.

"But this is wonderful," Dania said. "I'm more than happy for you right now," she hugged Ayesha ecstatically. "Have you told Amman about this yet?"

"I haven't had the chance of talking to him in the last few days. I'm a little worried too now." Ayesha seemed nervously happy.

"Don't worry. He'll call you. May be you should try again…"

Ayesha tried calling him, but Amman's number was switched off. It was a little strange for him, and Ayesha feared that something bad might have happened. She had absolutely no idea where and how Amman was. She spent the entire night looking out her window and staring at the moon, as if it would speak to her and tell her about Amman's whereabouts. She was lost in wonder. She kept reminiscing the time they had spent together in Himachal, how Amman used to hold her hand in the car, how he used to laugh and understood even the smallest of things that she refrained from saying out loud, and how they had chatted all the way back to Shimla, missing even the most beautiful of mountain sceneries outside. There were times when Amman used to look into her eyes for minutes at a stretch without uttering even a word. There was something nice about the time she had spent with him. She had never felt so at ease with anyone else in her life, the way she felt with him. She felt more at home with him. They had kissed each other, not at all times that they were together, nor had they made a habit out of it, for there was no need of it, but whenever she kissed him, there was something gentle and just right about it that was enough for her. The more she kissed him, the more she realized how wrong she had been with some of her preconceived notions about love.

She realized how she had misunderstood her father all her life. And now, when she looked at Dania, she realized that she was a girl with the same hopes and doubts as any other girl. And perhaps, she too wanted to marry the guy whom she had fallen in love with.

Chapter 12

It was the day of the wedding. Ayesha was in Dania's cottage as she got herself ready in the wedding dress Ayesha's father had brought for her. Rasheed had asked Javed not to bring an expensive dress and playfully chided him, saying, "Dania is my daughter first, then yours."

It was true, for since her childhood, Javed had taken up the responsibility of Dania's education and marriage. Both Dania and Ayesha went to the same schools and Dania was no less than Ayesha in terms of knowledge and intellect. They were almost equal.

"You look beautiful, Dania," Ayesha said.

Dania blushed. "You don't mean that."

"Yes," Ayesha said. "I do."

"Is he coming?" Dania asked curiously.

Ayesha shook her head and said, "I don't know."

"He might be stuck in some work, no?"

Ayesha nodded her head. "Come, let's go now," she said and took Dania's hand in her own.

The wedding proceedings were about to begin inside the *haveli*. All the guests mingled with one another all morning. They had all come dressed elegantly to the best of their capacity. They laughed and cracked jokes with each other. Most of them had drinks in their hands, but all non-alcoholic. A few servers carried around small platters of *kebab* and other finger foods for the guests to choose from, while a record played on the gramophone. The music was again *Sufi*, much to the liking of Ayesha's father as it had always been.

Javed made limited effort to engage with his guests, or rather, Rasheed's guests. He mostly limited himself to a corner, swirling his drink with a remote expression on his face. He smiled a courteous, close-mouthed smile whenever someone talked to him. Rasheed made sure that all his guests were comfortable and enjoying.

When the wedding ceremony began, Ayesha made sure that she was the one sitting alongside Dania throughout the proceedings. It was something she had never imagined would happen in her life, a day when they would both find themselves participating in a ceremony like this. That was her favorite part of the wedding, sitting next to Dania and watching everything happen before her eyes. It was nothing like what she had dreamt, but it seemed beautiful. Although she had been against marriage ever since her parents drifted apart, this celebration incepted the idea in her mind that there was indeed something which could complete her in a way she had never thought of. She thought of Amman and herself.

The guests seemed to be enjoying the wedding, judging by the nods and murmurs of approval around the hall where they were seated, and by their hearty applause when Dania and Ali, the groom, agreed to the union and said, "Yes" for marriage. In that moment, Ayesha could see the glee in Rasheed's eyes, and the joy on Dania's face. That was the one particular moment when she missed Amman's presence around her.

Once the wedding was over, Dania walked up to Ayesha who was standing all alone, staring at the entrance of the *haveli*.

"Are you okay?" she asked, concerned.

"I'm fine," Ayesha said, regaining her composure and flashing a smile on her face.

"Did he call?"

Ayesha shook her head.

"I'm sure he will come," Dania said.

"I suppose," was all Ayesha could say. She seemed disheartened. They walked back inside in silence.

"Do you think I did the right thing, Dania?" Ayesha stopped in her tracks and looked right at Dania.

"What do you mean?"

"You know, it was I who kissed him the first time…"

"So?"

"Do you think I made the right choice?"

"I'm not getting what you're trying to say, Ayesha," Dania held her hand.

"I think, I took the initiative and confessed my feelings to him first, before even knowing if he loved me back or not," Ayesha said, wondering herself where the conversation was headed.

"You are over-thinking it, Ayesha. You told me that he loves you, and he'll try and come for you. Is it not possible that he might have gotten stuck with some work at this time?" Dania squeezed her arm a little tighter and continued, "He'll come for you…if not today, then tomorrow. But he will."

Ayesha didn't say anything and simply looked at the ground. Dania lifted her face up by the chin and made her look into her eyes.

"After all that you've told me about him, I don't have even an iota of doubt on his loyalty. And yes, I've never been surer of anything for you, besides this guy. He's the one for you."

"But how can you be so sure of him? You have not even met him…"

"He's the best thing that has happened to you. Trust me!"

The moment Dania said this, Ayesha bowed her head and started to cry, leaning into Dania. Dania wrapped her arms around her, wondering what was wrong.

"I'm going to miss you, Dania," Ayesha said to her. She kept crying into her chest for what seemed like a long time.

Dania wasn't sure what to think, but said, "Although I've always missed you, I don't want you to ever lose him. I don't want you to say this for anyone ever again. Not even for me."

They both knew what *missing* meant, but Ayesha couldn't stop herself from saying it. Deep down, she knew that something inside her was lost permanently. Dania had been an important part of her life, but her going away now made things all the more solitary for her than before. Both of them shed some tears together, far away from the congregation. Dania told her that she would call her soon, after she settled in with her new family at her new home. She looked into Ayesha's eyes, and Ayesha saw genuine affection there for a sister. She touched Ayesha's face gently and said, "Make sure it's not too late for you."

Ayesha kissed the back of each of Dania's hands and uttered, "Dania, I wish you all the happiness."

Ayesha's father approached them just then, but averted his gaze when he saw them teary eyed. "Everyone's waiting for you, Dania," Javed said.

Ayesha wiped the tears off of Dania's face, and then her own.

"Yes, we're coming, dad."

She asked Dania if she was fine and Dania nodded.

That evening, Ayesha watched Dania leave the house they had grown up in. She slid into the backseat of the car, next to the groom, and looked out the window, stealing a last glance at all her closest family members. When her gaze landed on Ayesha, she pressed her palm against the glass. This was the last that Ayesha saw of her as the car pulled away from the driveway. Ayesha watched her go, her car turning at the end of the street, before Rasheed pulled the gates shut. Rasheed then hugged

Javed, and Ayesha saw his eyes moist for the first time in her life. She then went inside.

Later at night, she checked her phone for messages or phone calls, but there were none from Amman. She was highly disappointed that there had been no information from him regarding not coming. For the first time in her life, she felt alone in a way she had never found herself in. Dania had left now, Amman was not there with her, and the entire *haveli* seemed like an old abandoned place. She went into the dining room and sat at the glass table with her eyes closed. She remained there for a long time without moving and at some point, she heard some stirring upstairs. She blinked her eyes open and saw that the light outside had changed. She also found her father sitting next to her.

"Didn't you sleep last night, darling?" Javed asked.

"I didn't realize you were sitting here…"

"Well, I was here all the time." He asked Ayesha to go back upstairs and get some sleep.

"Are you embarrassed, dad?"

"What?"

"You know what I mean, don't you?"

"I don't know exactly…"

"Mother left you and then I didn't turn out as per your expectations. I'm sure you must be disappointed in both of us."

Javed did not say anything.

"Can I stay here for a few more days, dad?"

"You shouldn't," Javed said.

"I won't be long. Promise!"

"I'll stay here with you…"

"No, dad. It's just for a few days and I will be fine."

She wondered how many more times she was going to feel so broke and disheartened in her life. It felt as if life was only meant to disappoint her at every step.

"I don't know how you've decided to live your life, but don't make yourself like me. You won't be able to live like this for too long. This is not why I took you away from this place…you are my pride. Don't disappoint me there. I had made a decision," Javed said, "that I won't let your mother's absence influence you in any way, but you've chosen the same path. I'm not against your love, but you should know who you love well enough. You fell in love with someone unknown, a stranger, a nomad. You know they don't stay at one place for too long. You were only a passing fancy for him, I'm sorry to say this."

Ayesha didn't want to believe her father's words, but the circumstance she was in made it difficult for her to confront and negate them. She knew that he was not right, but it didn't make it any easier for her. She had made herself believe that she hadn't lost him entirely yet, that there still was some hope.

"Give me some time, dad. If what you say is true, I'll marry whomsoever you choose for me. But a few days is all I ask for." Suppressing her tears, she couldn't help but think about the worst.

"Take your time, but understand the consequences of the choices that you make in your life. It's only in the end that you'll start to feel their effects," Javed said and exited the room. She hadn't slept the night before and for the entire day after that. Her eyes were swollen from fatigue. She had gone from sadness to shock to denial to anger and then back again. All night long, she wished that whatever her father had said about Amman was not true, and prayed that the thoughts that had been annoying her for the past two days were nothing but a self-created nightmare.

Her fear, however, made her realize something else, something that made it all the more worse. She realized that she didn't know Amman all that well, but she had travelled with him for a month as if she had known him for long. The days she had spent with him were probably the most beautiful days of her life. Though she had fallen in love with him in only a month, those thirty days seemed like an entire lifetime. But when she thought about it now, all she could do was wonder how many more days she'd have to wait before seeing him again.

A couple of days later, Javed left Lucknow for Shimla again. Before leaving, he told her, "Come back to me soon." Ayesha could not lift her eyes to meet his, and simply nodded. He met Rasheed in private later that day and asked him to take care of Ayesha in his absence.

"I think you understand, Rasheed…something of what I'm describing to you. I know you do."

"Of course, I do," was all Rasheed said.

"Take care of yourself and Ayesha for whatever time she's here."

Naturally, he was going to. Javed made a request and Rasheed made his promise.

*****

Ayesha couldn't concentrate on anything for days. She made several phone calls to him, but none of her attempts was successful. She was worried at one point and infuriated at another. She woke up every morning hoping that there would be a call or message from Amman, but all her hopes turned into disappointments each time.

One day, she received a call from Nina. Ayesha told her all about Amman and the days they spent together in Shimla after she had gone back with Nihit. At first, Nina couldn't believe what Ayesha was telling her, as she had always known her as a very closed person who rarely spoke about her feelings. The brief affair that she had had with Amman surprised her in a big way.

Ayesha asked Nina if she had seen Amman in Shimla again, but her denial only added to her worries.

"You should come back, Ayesha. He'll come back for you," Nina said.

"I will. But this is not the time for me."

"You'll probably lose him if you stay there for too long. What if he comes looking for you back here? You won't even come to know," Nina said.

"People think I'm strange, don't they?" Ayesha asked.

"What?"

"Yes. Either I care for people too much or I don't care at all."

"Ayesha, people have different reasons. But shut the nonsense up and please come back here soon."

"I will," Ayesha said softly. "I'm very sick right now."

"So what? You'll take a few days, huh?"

Ayesha smiled tiredly. She knew what Nina was trying to say. She agreed to coming back and said, "But I'll take a few days here."

"Are you that sick already?" Nina asked.

Ayesha laughed, not knowing what to say.

"You're coming back within a week, Ayesha. I don't want to hear anything."

"Of course, I will."

*****

Ayesha kept herself locked in her bedroom for days. She walked out of her bedroom only to greet Rasheed once a day. This was not the first time for her. Something similar to this had happened a few years ago in London when another guy had left her, though she was not broken by it. She was still not broken, but something stopped her from coming out. She smoked cigarettes in her bedroom, closing all the windows and curtains so that Rasheed or the servants would not come to know about it. There were days when she did not speak to anyone except Rasheed, and wouldn't even change out of her sleeping gown. She did not eat properly some days, did not bathe the other, and this routine behavior from a girl like her caused Rasheed an uncharacteristic alarm.

After about two weeks of this, Rasheed knocked on Ayesha's door. He looked at Ayesha's disheveled hair and unkempt room when she opened the door. He sensed everything that was not right about it.

"I understand that you're not well these days," Rasheed said.

"It is not…"

"And I understand you consider me no less than your father…" Rasheed interrupted.

Ayesha lowered her gaze and spoke nothing.

"Go back to Shimla. I won't even ask what's wrong with you because I already know everything."

A startled expression washed across her face, the kind people have when a deep secret of theirs gets revealed in public without their consent.

"Did Dania tell you about it?"

"No. Your father did. He called me last week and told me everything. It's not only that the wait will not be worth it, but you're wasting your time here."

"I never wanted to be a disappointment like my mother, you know Rasheed uncle," Ayesha said.

"And always remember, it's never too late for anything in life. You don't have to be perfect, but you can always be good."

Ayesha closed her eyes and nodded.

"And I'm telling you this now," Rasheed said. "Please understand why I want you to go. Go and find yourself a life. Don't hide out here by yourself. Start a family. It's not too late, you know. There is still time for you."

"Well…" Ayesha said and stopped.

"You're blessed to have a father like yours who never stopped you from doing anything in life. So don't stay here for nothing. This is what I'm saying. Don't stay here for nothing. If you understand what I mean, then go find yourself a life."

Ayesha had never heard Rasheed say anything like that, and she understood that he was right. Rasheed kept his hand on her head and blessed her. Ayesha gave him a hug and promised him that she'd leave the next morning. And so it happened.

Ayesha packed her bags the same night and left for Shimla early the next morning after saying goodbye to Rasheed and thanking him for what he had said the night before. She knew that he trusted her with the decision that she was taking for herself, but things became a lot more obscure when she reached Shimla. She had not heard from Amman for almost a month now, and it bothered her to a great extent. She kept reminding herself how Amman had once said that no matter what, he would come back for her and only for her. She waited. At times, her inner self said something else, but she didn't want to arrive at any conclusions yet. She used to notice her father looking at her from a distance, but never said anything. It always disappointed her what she was doing to the people around her. She knew that her father had adopted a silence, but it was more of a punishment for her and made her feel quite embarrassed and guilty.

One day, her father approached her while she was sitting in the living room, reading a book. She looked at him and smiled cheerfully.

"Are you fine, darling?" Javed asked suddenly. Ayesha had been observing over the past few days that he was showing a certain concern for her which was very unusual to his nature.

"Everything is fine, I believe," she replied.

"How can you do this?" Javed asked. "How can you pretend that nothing is wrong?"

"I'm not pretending that nothing is wrong, dad. Haven't I always been like this?" she said and closed the book, waiting for an answer.

"I know. But this is different."

Ayesha wanted to evade the conversation, but calmed herself down. She started to feel betrayed by something, but did not want to blame Amman still. She remembered everything she had said to Amman, that this was the Lord's plan. *This*? She had never imagined all this, that too so soon. With Amman, she thought that the world belonged to them, but now even *that* world seemed nothing less than an illusion.

"Are you frightened?"

She wanted to say no, but looked away and said, "Yes. I'm frightened all the time. You never showed care for me throughout my childhood, but now you are showing concern for nothing all of a sudden."

"I am concerned for you all the time. I have always been. I just worry in private."

"I don't want you to worry about anything. Haven't we both lived our lives in loneliness? We both know that it can keep working the same way in future as well."

"But I'm not that young anymore, Noor. And I won't always be around. Get married." Javed had wanted to say *before I die*, but didn't.

"I don't want to get married right now. This is not the best time."

Ayesha believed that marriages happened all the time, even when they should not, and she had little faith in the institution of it. She believed in love, but the fate of love was something she was averse to. It had never unfolded in favour of her father, neither herself. That is what she believed, always finding herself on the wrong side of things.

"That guy you told me about has not made a single phone call to you, I know. Are you going to wait for him all your life?"

"I don't know," she said gently. "Maybe. I don't know what to do."

Ayesha felt numb even at the thought of being alone for the rest of her life. She stared at the dim light of her living-room. It was the end of January now and she had begun to feel that things were only going to get worse.

"I know this is hard for you," Javed murmured, "but there's nothing you can do." He looked at her with sympathy in his eyes. Ayesha kept quiet though.

"I don't know if there's anything I can say to you to make you feel good, but…"

"What should I do, dad?"

Javed drew closer to Ayesha and looked at her sadly. He put his arm around her shoulders and asked, "You really love him, don't you?"

Ayesha nodded and said, "With all my heart."

"And what's your heart telling you to do?"

"Maybe I should wait. Or maybe not…"

"Maybe you're trying too hard…"

"I don't know. I need some time perhaps," she said.

Ayesha looked out the giant windows of their living room at the mountains in the distance, in the hope that Amman would return someday. What she didn't know was how long she needed to wait.

By now, Ayesha had come to believe that some people had it easy in life. Everything they needed or wanted came easily to them, even though they might not have ever dreamt of it. And she knew love was one of those things for her, easy to attain for everyone but her. She didn't have it in her childhood, and only her Lord knew what her future held for her. What she did know was that the feeling of love could turn the world upside down and change things forever. She hoped that it wouldn't do the same sort of damage to her as it had done to her father. After all, everything in life was possible and attainable, but love was certainly not one of them. She believed that loving a person was the easiest and the most difficult thing in the world; a beautiful illusion in a way.

Days passed and Ayesha lost weight drastically. Her body seemed more fragile with each passing day. Although she had been having her food properly at regular intervals, something inside her was deteriorating her health. Her skin attained a slightly greyish tint and dark circles made a permanent place around her eyes. Her father chided her once, shaking his head at what she was doing with her own life. Despite all this, she looked beautiful.

"I'm doing okay, dad. There's nothing to worry about," was all she said every time her father asked her how she was doing. She flashed her near perfect smile with a twinkle in her eyes every time she crossed paths with her father.

"You should do something with your life, Ayesha. Other things can wait for now," Javed told her once while she was reading a book.

Then one day, she walked up to him while he was watching television and said frankly, "I was thinking of moving to Paris, dad."

"What?"

"Yes. Maybe for only a short period of time, but I'd like to do that."

"Have you lost faith?"

"It is not about that, dad. I'm not as weak as you think I am," she said. She knew she was lying, and that solitariness did bother her many times in that house. But she was losing a part of her own self with time.

"Is it because you think you might get better being there?" Javed again asked.

"No," she said. "It's because this seems to be the only right thing to do at this moment." *The right thing,* she remembered. "I'd like to go there and write. Besides, I need some time for myself far away from all this."

Her father turned his complete attention to her now. "Why Paris?"

"I don't know. I just feel like going there," she said softly. "And of course, I will return."

"Promise me that you'll be fine!" Javed said, his voice cracking a bit. "And you'll let me come see you if I want to…"

Ayesha nodded. "Just don't tell anyone where I'm going. It would be for the best."

Javed promised her that he wouldn't.

"And I will be back with you soon, dad."

"I'm sure you'll find some elegant way to hide whatever it is that you're trying to hide," Javed said before Ayesha left the room.

Ayesha sighed, looked away and left. She knew that things had transpired too quickly in the last couple of months. Things that she had never thought of had happened, and in such a hurry and confusion too. And just like that, without telling anyone about it, she left for Paris one day. Neither Dania, nor Nina and Nihit found out about it. She just left.

Chapter 13

"Just like that? I mean, she left for Paris without caring much about anything?" Jennifer asked.

"Yes, she did. I guess she did what any girl would have done in that situation. I tell you though, I've not seen another girl like her. She was different, a rare flower in the desert that one doesn't find easily. People can get very fragile and sensitive in the matters of love, and I believe she was one of them. She couldn't stay there for too long," Zafar said. He poured tea into a cup for Jennifer. Out of politeness, she took a sip.

"And then what? Did you meet Amman after that?"

"You know, sometimes it's not infidelity or betrayal that leads to a heartbreak. It's the circumstances also. It wasn't that she loved Amman any less or vice versa, but the situation made things worse for both of them," Zafar said and smiled. "Amman came back to Shimla then."

"Did he?" Jennifer asked, seeming curious.

"In a way no one had expected."

"What do you mean?"

"He had no spark of life left in him," Zafar said. "His mother had passed away."

Jennifer puffed her cheeks and let out the air slowly.

Zafar nodded. "That was the breaking point."

"I'm so sorry to hear that."

"Why would you be? But the person who needed to know this was not here anymore. Ayesha had already left for Paris. She had waited, but it was too late by then."

"I suppose," Jennifer said.

"You suppose?"

"No, of course. You're right."

"Look at it. It was no one's fault. But then, it happened and made things difficult for the two of them."

"I don't understand what that means," Jennifer said, a concern growing on her face.

"I believe when two individuals love each other way too much, there's bound to be a separation. And that's exactly what happened with the two."

"And what did Amman do then?"

"He made several attempts to search for Ayesha, sometimes by making trips to her house, sometimes waiting at my restaurant, but of course she was not there. Ayesha's father tried his level best to avoid Amman for a few days, but eventually…"

"He did, right?" Jennifer spoke excitedly.

"Well, one could say that. But you know how fathers are…"

"What did he say?"

"In the end, he lied to Amman, a lie which he didn't want to believe in," Zafar said and continued after a pause, "He told him that Ayesha had gotten married. And of course, he didn't tell him where she was."

"How stupid of him…" Jennifer uttered.

"I think someone had to play the devil here; first the circumstances, and then Ayesha's father. I tell you something, love is not for the romantics. It is rather for the brave ones."

Jennifer smiled. "Yeah, now I think I am beginning to understand it."

"Are you?"

"The way I see it from Ayesha's perspective, she was brave, no? Her entire life…what she had to live through from the very beginning…" Jennifer said.

"One could say that."

"And then?"

"Amman left for London, as he had once told Ayesha. But then, he left everything. Everything!"

"So they never met after that?"

Zafar nodded. "They did. Two years later, they did. In Paris."

Neither said anything for a few moments and watched the rain as it lashed against the window panes.

"When I told you that there's bound to be a separation when two individuals love each other," Zafar finally said, "what did you think I was talking about?"

Jennifer shrugged without answering.

"It only brings you closer."

CHAPTER 14

Ayesha was a gifted writer. She had written many poems over the years since her college days and a collection of poems got published in English and French. Although she was not very famous, the power and beauty of her writing was undeniable. She gave the account of her life in those verses she wrote, immortalised in the books forever. They were a well of words honest and lovely, at the same time brutal and sad. People felt enchanted by those poems as they connected with them. She was able to move her readers by conjuring emotions in their hearts that she had known herself.

It was in a café designed with a Moroccan decor, white drapes and black pillows everywhere, that she sat amongst an audience of a few people. She spoke about her writing journey to the low turnout. She had been to many book reading sessions now after having her poetry published, but there was always a certain discomfort she felt while among people. Reluctantly she accepted gifts from people, while declining many others. She always found it amusing and even endearing when people applauded her work, but then she also made sure that her personal life was never discussed. She was all too aware of the awkwardness that came with it. After many years, she was back to her usual resilient best, as she had been before. The old feeling of an absence in her life of something or someone vital had not dulled at all. It was still the same–of longing and missing. It still overpowered her now and then, even after two years, sometimes with a force that caught her unawareness; less frequently than it used to though. She was content, but not happy. Never again had she felt happiness the way she felt it with Amman two years ago.

Ayesha was not seeking answers anymore, but the feeling somehow kept coming back to her to go back to India for something that was not there for her anymore. She couldn't believe at times that two long years had disappeared in waiting for Amman, and in believing that he was not coming back to her for anything. The wait was both disturbing and annoying at times.

After she completed her reading session and a small conversation with the audience, she walked out of the café and lit a cigarette. She took a few drags from it and started walking west towards her apartment a few blocks away. She thought of calling her father that day, since she had spoken with him only once or twice in the last few days. While she walked, a girl stopped her to take a picture with her. She quietly obliged, gave her a peck on her cheeks and a fleeting hug. Ayesha walked on quietly, but soon spotted a figure across the street that seemed oddly familiar. Not for the first time, Ayesha's memory took her back to the days of cold winters spent in Shimla two years ago. As she neared the figure, she felt unsure whether that moment was real or in fact a memory, a ghost from the past of someone known.

She tossed her cigarette butt aside and looked at Amman. He stood tall in front of her. Shocked and surprised, she couldn't utter a word, but simply kept staring at him with a constant gaze.

"I did not expect to see you here…in Paris. Where have you been? I kept looking for you…" Amman said.

Ayesha still did not say a word, but rolled her eyes and shrugged genially. "Where did you expect to see me?" Ayesha said plainly. She didn't know how to react at that time. There was no sign of thrill or excitement in her upon seeing Amman after such a long time. She was surprised, but in a manner that did not generate any feelings of amazement in Amman himself. Ayesha rolled her eyes at him and gave him a drawn look. Her melancholy was like the darkness inside the coffee cup that Amman held in his hand.

It'd have been more fun had I seen you before. I'm glad you're here, Amman, but not very pleased, she thought. Her mind kept seeking ways to express her feelings, how she had been feeling over the last two years and how she was feeling now. "Do you know how I felt, Amman?"

"I looked for you all over Shimla and your father told me that you got married. Really? Couldn't you wait? Was I wrong to expect even a phone call or something from you?" Amman shuddered with a sudden jolt of anger.

"Why have you come now, Amman? Why now?" Ayesha asked with a minimum of surprise. "It's been two years. Didn't I wait for you? Didn't I deserve a message or a phone call when I waited for you at Dania's wedding? Not even after that?" Ayesha asked with no emotion in her voice. Her face was flat and her words had no feelings. Do y*ou know how every moment I have spent reminds me of you?* Ayesha kept thinking of all the things that she wanted to say the most, but did not. Her eyes grew moist after a moment, in a way that they hadn't in the last two years.

Amman nodded slowly. "Do you think it was planned?" Amman said.

"I'm sure, it wasn't. But then, I also turned out to be one of your passing fancies. You knew my heart, didn't you?"

"Why didn't you wait? Did a marriage mean so much to you that you couldn't wait for me, even when I had said I'd come for you?"

"For how long did you expect me to wait? I have been waiting for two god-damn years. There was no sign of you even after two months of the wedding that you were supposed to attend with me. I waited every moment, every minute of my life in the hope that you'd come, but you didn't. The only man whom I thought was always against my wishes proved me wrong; my father. When I told him about you, he didn't question me, not once. But you disappointed me. You broke whatever was left in me, Amman," Ayesha said and paused. "It's good to see you again. But tell me, why now?"

"Because I searched for you everywhere in the last two years, because I wanted to see you anyhow. Didn't I love you?" Amman's voice choked up as he spoke and the words rang with the most heartfelt emotion that he'd ever expressed. It took him a couple of minutes to finally get to the point. "I love you. I always have from day one. How I waited every single day to see you…" Amman took a pause suddenly and reminded himself that she was married. "I'm sorry. I forgot for a moment that you're now married. I am sorry. I got to know that you are in Paris through your book. I just couldn't stop myself from coming," Amman said.

Ayesha kept looking at him and thought if she should tell him the truth, but stayed quiet. They stood facing each other, but said nothing for a long time. Silence pervaded as both waited for the other to say something, for a miracle to happen, for the time lost between them to get restored, but silence was all. Neither knew what to say.

"We made a mistake, Amman. We should not make another by making false promises now. Remember, I said that I'd never want you to make me a promise. They always get broken somehow. I'm glad we didn't make any of those. It saved both of us a lot of regrets."

"Do you have any regrets?" Amman asked her.

Ayesha's face grew pale and her body felt feather light. Of course, there was a certain joy inside her, but she suppressed all those feelings in hope of saving herself from a lot of melodrama that could happen.

"We all have regrets, Amman," she said. "I don't regret the time when I met you though. That was wonderful."

"Why would you say that now?"

"Because I loved you too," Ayesha cried out, unable to hide her anguish. "That," she admitted, "...was better. The best."

"And now you don't?" Amman asked.

"This is not the time, Amman. And I'm sorry."

Amman nodded.

"But other than that, I was happy. I really was." Despite her tears, she laughed and felt guilty for doing so immediately. "I'm happy because I fell in love with someone and had him love me back."

Amman kept staring at her without saying anything. There was silence between the two, an awkward silence even in the crowd on the road. *That's what distance always brought between lovers,* she thought.

"Can you stop loving someone just because of some distance brought in between by the circumstances?" Amman asked and looked at her, knowing full well that she loved him still, as she kept quiet and had conflicting emotions reflect in her eyes. He couldn't blame her for staying quiet, not really. He knew how Ayesha had lived her entire life. In silence.

"I don't know what I'm supposed to say anymore..."

"Do you think we met in those mountains for nothing?" Amman asked again.

It was the first time he had demanded an answer from Ayesha, but these were unusual times.

"I'm not sure I understand what you're asking," Ayesha said.

"You do..."

"No, I don't," she interrupted, frowning. "I don't. But I know I'm doing the right thing now. I know that something's missing in my life, but I can't stay with you right now. You think if I spend time with you, you'll bring back the time we've lost? You think everything's going to be okay?" Ayesha paused and turned away, crying. "I don't want you to do anything anymore. I don't know if there's anything more that you can do at all. The more you try, the more hopeless things will seem to me."

"Is there any way to stop why you feel this way?" Amman already knew by then that Ayesha was not coming back to his life and he would only receive despair in return.

She turned to look at him and said, "Amman," she almost pleaded, "No, there is not. And I'm helpless."

"You're not helpless, Ayesha. You're frightened…"

"I know, and even though you're trying…things will continue to get harder and harder for both of us. And I don't want you to try. I don't want you to try."

Amman stood there for a long time, thinking how much he loved her. A part of him wanted to cry right there, but he held her hand close to his heart instead, feeling the warmth of her fingers, and pulled her closer.

"Let me go, Amman," Ayesha said softly. "Leave me…"

Amman moved an inch closer and looked into her eyes, saying, "I am."

He let go of her hand, looked at her for a moment, then walked away without turning back.

Eventually, the fight ended. Despite Amman's attempt of persuading her to come back to him, Ayesha didn't give in to her own feelings and had stayed firm. She was confused and worried at what she had done. The moment Amman disappeared into the crowd again and could not be seen, Ayesha's mind flipped into the past and Dania's words echoed in her head, *He's the best thing that has happened to you. Trust me. I want you to never lose him.*

"But I've lost him, Dania. I lost him a long time ago," she mumbled to herself and tears leaked from her eyes.

That night, back at her apartment in Paris, she felt aimless and adrift. Something struck her really bad that same night. She received a long distance phone call, all the way from India. She had not expected a call at that time of the night. It was eleven in the night and only a few people, her friends from Paris itself, called her that late. Prior to the call, Ayesha had been sobbing alone in her room, having no idea about what was coming her way. She had not even prepared any food for herself that night. When the phone rang, she wiped her tears and picked up the receiver to hear a man's voice on the other end. She greeted the person in French, "Monsieur…" and continued to speak in French until she realized that the person on the other end was not saying anything.

"I'm sorry, but may we speak in English or Hindi?"

"My apologies. Of course…we may speak in Hindi. I assumed…anyway, may I know who it is?"

"Ayesha, it's me, Rasheed."

Ayesha was shaken. It had been two years since Dania got married, and Ayesha hadn't spoken to her or even Rasheed in all this while. She wondered how time had gone by in regret, memories and guilt.

"Is Dania fine?" Ayesha spoke fast without even listening and felt guilty at how bad she was in keeping up with people who had raised her and loved her unconditionally.

"It's your father, I'm afraid," Rasheed said from the other end.

"I'm sorry?"

"He's no more," came the voice from miles away and jolted her deep inside. It was perhaps the biggest jolt of her life.

Rasheed went on about how bad his health had gotten in the last few days, and that he had been with him for the past week, but Ayesha heard none of it. Her hands were shaking. A part of her wanted to hang up, as she could not endure listening to what Rasheed was telling her, giving her the account of Javed's last days. Her pulse fluttered and palms became sweaty. She thought of hanging up, but Rasheed soon asked, "When was the last time you spoke to him?"

"A week ago," Ayesha said. She was numb by then and there were no tears in her eyes. A moment of silence settled between the two before Rasheed said, "Ayesha…"

"I will be there soon," Ayesha interrupted and hung up. At that moment, a startling realization hit her that how trivial her existence had become and how alone she was in the entire world. The image of her father sitting on his recliner, or alone in his study, listening to *Sufi* music which he was very fond of resurfaced in her mind. She also thought of some truly remarkable moments from her childhood. Memories rose up from the depths of her subconscious mind to strike her–Lucknow, her father, Dania, Rasheed picking her up from school, her mother's face which had faded with time, and some particular memories of her. She gazed out of her window in the direction of the Eiffel tower where the lights were coming from, and wondered whether there was anyone in the world whom she could call her own. All her existence had come to a zero in the end. Something inside her wished for Amman to be with her at that moment, but all she could see out the window was an elusive shadow. A figure. She searched for his face and remembered his once soft hands holding hers, but it evaded her, slipped from her mind each time she turned to it. Ayesha felt a deep void now, as if a life of her own had vanished with her father's demise; a great absence. All that echoed in her mind were words said by people to her.

"Amman," she said, unaware that she was speaking, also unaware that she was weeping.

She sat on her bed, not knowing what she could do at that moment. She waited for the evening to fade away so she could see the dawn again. She shut her eyes and found herself back at the haveli in Lucknow at once. The hills of Shimla stood tough, blue and sky-high outside the window as the sun set behind them. Her memory juggled between the two places, there where she had once lived and that which never left her sight, no matter what part of the world she lived in.

*****

Back in Lucknow the next day, Ayesha stood next to the window and looked outside. She didn't know what to think and what to believe, but she stood still as if contemplating something serious. Her life seemed like a parody to herself, a melodrama of shackled beauties and doomed romances, and depression. An amalgamation of all, told in a breathless and high spirited fashion. The sky outside darkened rapidly, and a sudden downpour lashed down heavily, rippling over the windows and smearing the headlights outside. Ayesha had never imagined that she would be all alone in her life one day with no one around to take care of her, that her entire life would consist of memories alone, whether joyous or tragic. Just like her father, she had her own ideas and was now a woman rightfully worried over the well-being of a deeply unhappy and self-destructive lady she was going to become.

Rasheed entered her room at that moment. He asked her how long she had planned to stay there for.

"I'm probably not going anywhere now," Ayesha said.

Rasheed nodded.

"May I ask you something, Rasheed uncle?" Ayesha asked and turned to him.

"Please!"

"What do you think of my father's relationship with mother?"

"Why are you asking this now?"

"I wouldn't know otherwise," she said. "I never asked anyone else in this house, but I want to know now because it matters to me."

"I like to believe that your father loved your mother very much. It's a different thing altogether that they didn't live with each other their entire life, but I'd still like to believe so."

"Why?"

"I had seen it in his eyes. Though he felt betrayed by what your mother did, it never stopped him from loving her. I've always known one thing to be true; no matter how much you curse your love for its consequences, it still makes things beautiful and no one has ever escaped it."

"I suppose."

"You suppose?"

"Well, all my life, I've cursed people because I always felt unwanted, but here I am. Father was always so important in my life, although I never said this to him. People whom I've loved have always left me for no reason."

"Do you really think so?" Rasheed asked.

Ayesha began to cry. "I'm sorry," she whimpered through her ragged sobs. "I'm so sorry…"

"I've come to know a little about this guy you love, through your father. And I believe, if that guy loves you, you must go to him. I know it may not be the priority right now in your mind, given the situation, but it is the most important thing in life. Love is the most important thing in life…above everything else. Very few get this privilege, and your father was the unlucky one."

It took another long moment for Ayesha to stop crying, and she looked up at Rasheed. He kissed Ayesha's forehead, almost like the breath of a passerby on a city street, then placed his hand on her head, blessing her.

"I do not say this with authority, but find where you belong. You must find your truth and love wherever it is."

A sad smile flashed across Ayesha's face, and she knew what he was trying to tell her.

"You must go, Ayesha."

The next day, she took a flight to Bombay and reached Amman's house where his mother lived. Before reaching Bombay, she had told herself that she wouldn't bring the past back up and would start afresh. She decided that she would talk to him like she did all those years ago, and would do everything possible to make things better. The silence of more than two years might have taken away the pain of distance, she thought. She decided to tell him everything about the time she had spent in solitariness, and the love that had never died in her for him. Little did she know that fate had decided to show her something else entirely.

Ayesha had never been to Bombay in her life before, but somehow managed to find where Amman's mother lived. He had once told her about the school where she taught and where she lived. When Ayesha found the building, she felt a sudden surge of anxiety and a strange feeling, as if she was not ready for what was coming. She ascended the stairs of the building and reached the second floor, wiped her forehead and rang the doorbell of the apartment. A man opened the door and looked at her with an unfriendly, rather remote and impenetrable, expression. He was taller than her, had broad shoulders, thin lips and a shiny forehead. He had on a white shirt and glasses over his eyes. Ayesha greeted him.

"Yes?" the man asked.

"I believe, a lady used to live here…Amman's mother?"

The man gazed at her for a brief moment, then asked, "Who are you?"

"I'm Amman's friend. I have come to see his family…his mother in particular," Ayesha said.

"I'm sorry, but they don't live here anymore. His mother died some time ago," the man replied with sympathy growing in his eyes.

"But she lived here, didn't she? I mean, not very long, but…"

This information had come as an extreme shock to her, and her mouth remained open. Her mind had multiple things running simultaneously regarding what might have happened in the last couple of years, where Amman could be now, and her biggest fear–if she had lost him forever.

"Yes, she did. But she passed away two years ago, I believe. Amman left this apartment right after that."

"Do you know where he might be now?" Ayesha asked immediately.

The man shrugged. "Well, no."

"Do you know any of his immediate family members or someone by whom he could be reached?"

"I'm afraid, no."

Silence followed. The man closed the door after that, without saying anything. She found herself thinking back to the conversation she and Dania had had two years ago at her wedding. The words kept coming back to her, *Don't lose him!* She missed everything now, the mattress she had shared with him two years ago in the mountains, the road journey she had taken with him two years ago in the mountains, her first kiss at midnight, the Christmas she had celebrated with him on their last night together, and the jumble of memories of the time past which always poked her. She missed all of it. She missed her father now, missed Dania, and her friends Nina and Nihit. Never before had she ached so badly for home.

It was the moment when she sensed that life could be treacherous if you loved it way too much, while happiness was a guest which always knocked at your door unexpectedly. Sadness, though, lingered longer than the joys in life. She understood now that all the lives that had touched her had a trajectory quite different from hers. She wondered now whether meeting Amman was only a chance and not her destiny, and that patience and love could deceive you with the surprises of life. Her fate had only led her to the different turns of life which she had never imagined encountering.

While she stood in the crowded street of Bombay in autumn, she looked up to the sky and wailed. As the raindrops fell on her face, she closed her eyes in regret, and regret alone.

Chapter 15

5 years later

London

Editor's Note

(Magneto), P.7

Dear readers,

Five years ago, when we began our quarterly issue featuring interviews with little-known writers from around the world, we could not have anticipated how famous they all would become at some point. We remember how our readers asked for more interviews with such writers, and their enthusiastic response allowed us to go forth with our feature interviews. They were not famous personalities when we began; some of them are still not, as they prefer to keep a low profile, despite the success they enjoy in their profession. A few of those writers have become our editorial staff's personal favorites, and one of them is Amman. In the last few years, we have discovered many writers and artists. Some of our features have even led to the re-discovery of some great writers and have bestowed upon their work an appreciation long overdue. But Amman was already a sensation since his first book, and then the startling success of his love trilogy. A first hit could easily have been a fluke, but three consecutive successful books in five years had to be accounted for in our quarterly edition. Ironically, a shadow hovers over his personal life, and we could not ignore the various letters from his fans requesting us to carry a feature story on him. The artist featuring in this quarter's edition is Amman himself. He's a man who has risen to a great height with his work, and we're sure that our feature will carry one of the most honest and revealing interviews with him, as we always deliver.

*****

"You don't actually read all this, do you?" asked Robert.

"Sometimes!" Amman said, as he kept the magazine back on the table.

"It's pathetic how they describe everything in the newspapers and magazines. I wonder how they've managed to survive after all these years." Robert Tanner was Amman's agent in London who had helped him a few years ago in getting a contract with a leading publishing house in London. He was forty, and Amman didn't miss a chance to teased him every time he tried to look cool and young.

"When are you leaving for India?" Robert asked as he poured himself a glass of wine.

"Tomorrow," Amman said.

"After five years, isn't it?" Robert raised his glass in the air and said, "Cheers!" He took a sip then and said, "This is a new house."

It was Amman's ordinary two bedroom apartment in London where he had settled full time three years ago, having left India and his job of a travel writer.

"Tell this to the owner then," Amman said.

"Aren't you the owner? I always believed so..." He was sitting on a chair in the balcony facing the street.

"I may leave London for good once I come back from India."

"Have you gone entirely mad, huh? You'll leave everything you've achieved here?" Robert asked, swirling the wine in his glass.

"I've lived here for too long, way beyond my own expectation."

"And where are you heading to after this?"

"I've no idea," Amman said laughing.

"Do you have any idea of what you'll lose here?"

"I'm aware of what I've achieved here."

Robert nodded.

"I know that you've been of great help to me here. I've found a friend in you…"

"Probably just like many others in your nomadic life. I'm not surprised," Robert said and sipped some more wine. "I think you've not been able to leave some part of your life before coming here. You know, the life you lived in India before all this happened here. You still travel, but only to be lost somewhere. The difference now is that you're not trying to explore anything…"

"A little bit," Amman said, "If you say it, I believe you."

"And what about the girl? What if you see her in India?"

Amman nodded heavily. "I believe it's not happening anytime soon. The last I saw her, she was in Paris. I remember clearly. And I've no idea where she could be now."

"It's been five years now, Amman. People may not know it, but I'm not just your agent here. I'm your friend too. You don't have to hide anything from me," Robert said. "You see, time is like a wheel. It always comes back in some way or the other to begin a new circle," Robert smiled.

Amman nodded and smiled back.

"All I know is that she married someone…"

"That's a lie. You already know it."

Amman shook his head. "But it's been years now. Time changes a lot of things in life, not to mention the circumstances."

Robert groaned and placed his glass of wine on a table next to him. "Well, then why do you still wait for her?"

"I don't. Besides, there's a time for everything in life. That time didn't belong to us."

"But this could be. Mark my words!"

Amman sat beside him, ice tinkling in his glass now. His feet were bare. "There isn't a day when I don't think about her. It doesn't help anyway, Robert."

"Well, at least you're honest," Robert said. "At least you are honest."

"How could anyone lie about love?"

Robert smiled at him. "Oh, I'm glad that love hasn't died after all these years…"

"It never did. Did you think so?"

"What?"

Amman looked at him as if Robert hadn't understood what he meant.

"You might not have understood it, but yes, it didn't."

They drank some more wine and talked for some time, their first genuine conversation since Amman's arrival in London, free of all the subtle mocking, publishing-related hassles, his vague approach to life that he had sensed in all these years of knowing him. Robert was a guy married twice. He had been divorced when they met for the first time, and looked older than what he actually was. Over the next five years that Amman had known him after that, his appearance only went from bad to worse.

"Oh, you always mock me, man…"

"And don't you think you're still young? You're just past forty," Amman teased him.

"A little bit," Robert said. "I'm not that old. I'm still capable of marrying someone." He tapped Amman on his shoulder playfully and said, "I worry about you though."

"You don't need to start again."

"I'm not," Robert said

"You don't stop sometimes."

"But tell me, where will you move to after London?" Robert asked.

"Haven't figured that out yet," Amman said. He paused before adding, "I will perhaps spend some time in India."

"Good for you," Robert said. "Sounds a fine idea. Tread carefully though."

"We are never meeting in real life again, but…" Amman said and they shared a brief grin.

"Will you be all right?"

"Yes, in the short term," Amman whispered slowly.

*****

Later, when Robert had left, Amman sat in the living room and called Zafar in India. He realized that his life had somehow trodden down its own path, different from what he had thought it would be. Now, it entreated him to go back to where everything had started. It was, however, difficult for him to go back to the place where there was no one whom he could call his own. *What madness*, he said to himself. He was sad that he could not see his mother now, his friends that had gotten left behind years ago, and his love Ayesha. He made sure that he would be able to separate himself from the swarming horde of people at the launch of his book there, but also knew that things would get worse for his own self.

"Are you sure you're coming?" Zafar asked for the hundredth time, not realizing that Amman had called him after three whole years.

"Time will fly. I'll come and see you soon," Amman said.

"You won't have to go to Shimla now. I've shifted to Delhi."

They talked about a few other things about his stay in New Delhi and the places all over India where he was going for a promotional tour. At one point, Amman could think of nothing more to say and just watched the stars outside his window. Zafar comprehended the silence that had fallen between them and asked, "Did you hear anything from her?"

Amman refused.

"Well, there's someone here waiting for your arrival, someone who believes she can write a story on you."

"Do you really think so? I think it can wait for now."

"She already knows a lot about you, through me of course. But I think if she could just meet you in person once, she'd be done with her job," Zafar insisted. "Just meet her once."

"I hope so. Although, I don't believe this is even a story to read."

"She needs to have it. She has come all the way from London, can you believe it?" Zafar laughed.

"That's poor, when she could easily have seen me here in London. It sure would have saved her a lot of time."

"Odd way of marketing, I guess," Zafar mused. "I believe they know over there that you don't do all these interviews…"

"Did you tell her this?"

"No."

"Then I hope she'll be all right," Amman said and smiled mildly.

Amman could practically hear Zafar laughing his squeaky laugh somewhere miles away over the phone. One thing Amman had come to terms with was that nothing in life ever stopped for him. It did make some things painful for him, but the recognition that came along with it had never crossed his mind before. Even after all this time, solitariness was one thing he could always trust, unlike people. He believed that people always became what they became because of the circumstances they lived through and not something they were born with. He understood it well that whatever had happened between Ayesha and himself a few years ago was only because of the state of affairs they were both in at that time. He knew whatever he did had been the right thing to do indeed, but he had missed someone's presence at every step of his life. Ayesha was the best girl he had met in his life, especially considering how natural things had been between them. It was only time that had done what nobody else or no other thing could between them. There was a time when he had prayed for a miracle. They supposedly happened all the time, as he had read so many times. He had used these words in his writing too. But unfortunately, he had never witnessed such a thing in his own life. Every day, he was reminded that the world had less miracles and more misfortunes. The thought had clung to him like a never ending dark night, hopeless of a dawn.

There were days when he visited a church near his apartment. He somehow felt it to be the right thing to do. Although he had lost all hope of seeing Ayesha ever again in his life, his heart still told him that there could be something more to look forward to. This was all that he wondered the most at night. Other times, he'd sit on his empty couch and look at the stars in the distance, thinking of her happy face and wondering whether she had found someone, forgetting the agony of her lonely childhood.

He remembered how Ayesha had once told him to spend his holidays anywhere but in London because it was so boring, and that she would take him to a place they would cherish forever. He often laughed at himself for how he had landed in London, leaving the entire world behind. Most of his thoughts revolved around Ayesha and his mother. It was in moments like these when he thought too much about them, and if someone came up to him asking about his silence, he always withheld the details of his life, especially from India before London. He kept people at bay from his past, but people were people, they never stopped asking. The more popularity he received around the world with his books, the more people got interested in his life, but he never gave them any piece from his life.

He wondered if there was a greater lesson in what was happening with him in life. And if this was all, as Ayesha had once said, simply a part of the Lord's plan? Had the Lord wanted him to fall in love with her? If yes, why were they not together? The answers to such questions were not clear to him. He figured that it was the right time for him to leave for India.

Outside, the last of the dark had passed. It had been a gloomy night, but the morning light was breaking through the clouds. In the cool spring air, he could see the first signs of nature coming back to life. The trees outside were budding, as if they had been waiting for the right moment to unfold all the mysteries of life, and open themselves up to another season of love.

"It's time. Get yourself ready," Robert said, as he called Amman early in the morning.

"Robert?" Amman said softly.

Robert didn't answer, but Amman went ahead saying, "I'd like to be left alone…"

"I'd like to talk to you," Robert said firmly.

"Please," Amman said. He sounded defeated by his tone, as though he didn't have the strength to confront even Robert.

Robert listened as he told him what was on his mind. When Amman finished, Robert simply said after a pause, "You should go."

CHAPTER 16

Excerpts From an Interview With Amman by Jennifer Kohl (Magneto), P.26

The man sitting across from me wears his celebrity lightly. He is open and friendly, and perhaps the warmest person I've met in all these years. And yet, many in the literary world harbor the misconception that he is distant, even arrogant. As I met the charming Amman at his hotel room in New Delhi, I realize to my surprise that many out there made the same mistake when they first met him, as told to me by Amman himself.

A: It has always been like this. Your silence is always considered to be a sign of your arrogance, which in most cases is not true at all.

JK: But you really surprise me, especially after what I heard from Zafar, your friend here.

A: He did tell me about you.

Amman smiled and shrugged at this.

JK: I am struck by your choice of career, given that you spent the early years of your life as a traveler in India.

A: I don't know. Something at that point made me want to escape everything that life had to offer me, especially after my mother died.

JK: And Ayesha also happened to be at that point in your life where you both drifted apart.

A: In some way, yes.

JK: Was that thc point when you took to writing too?

A: Precisely, yes. Although, what followed after that was something I had not expected. I took to writing as a personal interest. I was already writing for my publishers as a travel writer, so I guess it was all about writing a story now in a fictional format.

JK: And are you happy now?

A: Entirely depends on how you want to see it.

JK: You don't approve of all this, do you?

A: Whether I approve or not is irrelevant. These are stories that I'm writing. Lives of people don't depend on it.

I asked him to tell me about his early life. He gave me a narrative of his childhood and how he decided to travel the world all by himself. He also told me a bit about his father.

A: My father, he was very stern when I saw him three years ago in London, after my mother died. All these years, I had so much of this rage in me that he had left both of us when I was only five. But when I met him, I realized that he regretted the decision he had taken. He was a man full of remorse and he told me, *be everything in life, but not a man with remorse.* I think he quite understood now what it meant to lose someone, when I told him about mother.

JK: Then why did he leave her in the first place?

A: I think it was one of the decisions he took after a small scuffle with her when I was still very young, that he had made a mistake marrying her while they were both at a young age.

JK: I've come to see that there's a lot of similarity in the stories between the girl you loved and you own!

Amman smiled again.

JK: So, you didn't see much of him. He was an absentee figure for a major part of your life.

A: Entirely.

JK: And now? Have you kept in touch with him after that?

A: Not much. He used to come to my apartment back in London once in a while to spend some time with me. He would come and tell me how he missed everything in his life. But something inside me could never accept the unsaid apology on his face. He's still in London.

JK: How had you mother coped with him leaving?

A: She was strong. I have never seen a woman as strong as her in my entire life. My upbringing was everything that mattered to her. Since she was a teacher, she inculcated strong values and emotions in me, and to not give up easily in life. She taught me about love in its purest form–not to seek it, but to spread it. There's a reason I could do everything in have done in life. It is because her love was always with me no matter where I was. Unfortunately, she died too soon. She was only fifty-five. I never saw her dejected, at least in front of me. She was a woman full of life. Imagine, a woman, not even divorced, not being loved by anyone, yet so strong and lively. That's a rare quality you'll ever find in anyone.

JK: She was a woman par excellence.

A: I wonder if she was told this by anyone in her life.

JK: But she was, I gather.

A: I believe relationships aren't always meant to end on a happy note. I'm sure my parents loved each other, but probably could not keep up with the unwanted things that often creep into every relationship, especially my father.

Amman poured me a cup of tea. Out of politeness, I took a sip. He didn't say anything for a while. I stopped the recorder I was carrying meanwhile.

JK: It also brings me to Ayesha. What happened to her?

He smiled wryly.

A: I assume you've already been told a lot of it by Zafar.

JK: I prefer to hear the story in your words though.

A: And all this time, I thought I was telling you the story in my words.

JK: Naturally. But I'd like to hear it from you now, not from a third person.

He chuckled.

A: It is like any other story. You know how people meet and then drift apart naturally. It happened the same way with us. That was the difficult part. To lose her over something I didn't even have any control.

JK: I guess, we always lose people when we don't have control over something, isn't it?

He smiled a little sadly. He offered me a sandwich, which I decline at this point. He asked me if I was married. I told him I am not and perhaps would never be. He looked at me and grinned.

A: Why not?

JK: It's hard to find love these days.

A: What I can tell you, however, is that whenever you find it, you must make a decision.

JK: I suppose that'll never happen. Look at your own story, or the people around. Your father left your mother, Ayesha's mother left her husband and you…you also did not find one for yourself.

I realized the crudeness of what I had just uttered.

JK: I'm sorry.

A: You miss the point here.

JK: What?

A: They all loved each other. Though obviously, they were not together.

JK: And you believe in stories like these?

A: I would answer in the affirmative. I am not trying to be modest about any of it, or being an apologist for love. But I've realized that the feeling of love never ceases to be, no matter what part of the world you live in. I also believe that when there is too much love between two people, they fail to keep it alive between them.

JK: But that's devastating, don't you think so? A love like this…

A: As I understand, yes.

JK: And I came to know that the girl you loved was a poet herself.

A: And much better at creating than any of what I've written so far.

I assume that this was his honest assessment of his own writing. False modesty is not his suit. He broke in poems written by the girl herself, making use of his free-flowing memory. I realized that her writing was indeed groundbreaking.

JK: You remember her poems?

A: I got to read her work only after it got published, like many others. Her poetry doesn't speak of any high and lofty notion about art, but her own pain that she has suffered through life.

JK: Do you think she has mentioned you in any of her poems?

He kept quiet for a moment.

JK: You don't have to answer this.

I suppose it displeased him.

A: I believe, through art of any kind, you express yourself in an abstract manner. You do everything in your capability, but leave it for the others to understand and interpret. In love, you express yourself freely, you make someone else's dreams and desires your own without filtering out their flaws. You accept their sufferings and hurt as your own. Everything knowingly too! You do not love people by practically weighing their flaws and perfections, but foolishly. If love isn't foolish, it isn't love.

JK: Forgive me for saying this, but you two didn't end up together.

A: If two people do not end up together, does that make their love any less?

JK: I'm sorry to say it, but this love doesn't feel right.

He laughed his delightful laugh, though his eyes spoke something else entirely. There is a cunning intelligence about them.

A: I agree with what you say. It doesn't feel right to me either.

JK: Then do me a favor. Tell me that you still love her at least.

A: I thought that was the only reason why we are here.

JK: So you do?

A: Do I have to say the words out loud? Of course, I do.

I felt sorry for him.

JK: Then why didn't you ever go back to her?

A: If I had, you wouldn't be here. It thickened the plot, though.

I laughed. He smiled.

JK: You love her. How could you have let go of her so easily?

A: In hindsight, I realize that this is how it was supposed to be. We just couldn't be together then. There were no promises made, no dreams of eternity. I think that was the reality of it, but whatever we shared between us was all true.

JK: I'm not surprised!

I realized at this point that despite whatever Amman said, or however sensible he seemed by the words he uttered, he still missed the love of his life. Sadness emerged on his face every now and then, but he hid it behind the web he created with the stories. I honestly was disappointed for all the discordance I felt in his views. I told him this freely.

JK: I'm sorry, but I'm already too much into your story, and I'm a bit disappointed.

A: Why?

JK: Because I see the love, but not the longing in your eyes.

A: You know, I always used to say that there's a right time for everything in life. Had I been with her at that point of time, it wouldn't have worked. I didn't want for either of us to remain shackled to the other for years. We were both living a time that didn't belong to us.

JK: And what would you've done had it happened today?

Needless to say, he smiled again, albeit a little sadly.

A: I wouldn't have let her go.

JK: May I ask if you're still hopeful of seeing her?

I believe he took a moment to retrospect, then said, "Life is too long to feel the guilt, or to continue missing someone. I'm done doing that, I think."

He left me baffled with that statement, and probably read my mind.

A: I will see her again. I'm not sure when and where though…

*****

When Amman walked out of the hotel, he didn't care how he looked, as he suspected people wouldn't care either. He slowed down and tried to remind himself of the days that had been left behind. He looked up at the sky as he heard the clouds thundering and lightning. He kept walking at a slow pace, and it started raining heavily within a few seconds. He smiled as it reminded him of the rain in which he had first seen Ayesha years ago in Shimla. He spotted a church a little distance away from where he stood and rushed towards it, dodging the hurrying people on the footpath and narrowly escaping getting hit by a car on the road.

When he finally entered the church, he slowed down his pace again and tried to catch his breath. He found the church entirely empty, sans even the priest. Papers were scattered across the benches and copies of the Bible were strewn around as if no one had straightened the place up for days. Subconsciously, he started putting the place in order.

"Excuse me?" Amman heard a soft voice. "Is father here?"

Amman didn't answer, but turned to see who had called. The face looked older, but beautiful as ever, just as he had seen it the first time seven years ago. Ayesha saw him now, but was too shocked to speak. Amman marched right up to her and glanced at her before turning back to the altar and smiling. Ayesha couldn't take her eyes off of him. They were both nervous and it took them a couple of minutes to finally acknowledge each other's presence. Ayesha felt her voice choked with emotion as she tried to speak.

"When I asked you to promise that you won't fall in love with me, why did it hurt me?"

Amman shrugged and answered, "It was impossible to not fall in love with you."

He apologized for his disheveled appearance and thanked Lord for the first time. The words just came out of the mouth of a never-going-to-church man. Ayesha looked pale, but still had a gleam in her eyes and a smile which told him that she had fought the same things that he had struggled with in his recent past.

"Thank you for coming back," Ayesha said.

"I'm sorry. I just couldn't help it back then."

That was the moment he cried out in front of Ayesha, unable to hide his anguish. Ayesha took his hands in her own, her grip strong, and smiled tenderly at him.

"This," she admitted as she looked into his moist eyes, "could be better."

Amman looked at Ayesha's face and noticed that it had grown leaner, her hair had lost its lustre, yet her eyes, those soft brown eyes, were as lovely as ever.

"I don't think I've ever seen someone as beautiful as you."

"How can you say that? I'm a complete mess."

Despite the tears in their eyes, they both laughed.

"Perhaps I can tell Dania now that I've fallen in love and have someone to love me back."

Amman kissed her hand when she said that and held it against his cheek.

"Do you have any regrets now?" Amman asked again, the way he had in Paris five years ago. He wanted to tell her his thoughts, but the sound of her voice suddenly silenced the emotions inside him.

"We all have regrets, Amman," Ayesha said. "But I don't want to say this to myself ever again."

Amman couldn't understand what that meant.

"Do you love me?" Ayesha asked him.

Amman smiled. "Yes."

Ayesha leaned forward and kissed Amman. "I love you too," she whispered.

These were the words Amman had been hoping to hear again for a very long time. Finally getting control of himself, he kissed her again, brought his hand to her face, and gently brushed his fingers over her cheek.

He gazed at her gentle eyes, her hair and gushed at the softness of her skin. A lot of memories from the past flashed before his eyes, and a future seemed certain now. Without thinking much, he felt the urge to do something that he probably had never imagined he would do. It was his heart which told him to do so. He smiled softly, looked into her eyes with affection, took a deep breath and asked, "Will you marry me?"

Ayesha emptied her chest with a long sight and smiled.

About the Author

Amit Sharma is a published author & poet of two works titled, *White Feathers* and *My Elementary Life*. He has also written two short stories titled *Still Loving You* featured in **Half-baked stories** in collaboration with 17 other writers from all over India, and *You Are the One* published on Juggernaut's writing platform. At present, he's working on his fourth book which is a non-fiction. In 2017, his poetry collection, *My Elementary Life* was reviewed by **Kitaab**, a publishing house based in Singapore. He also likes to paint sometimes and did theatre for a short span of time in New Delhi with Asmita Theatre Group.

He lives in Gurgaon with his family.

Reach him at:

Instagram: sharmamiit

Email: amitsh5201@live.com